An ingenious tightly plotted suspense the
As with a thriller, there is pleasure to be had
here in trying to predict the turn of events"
TIMES LITERARY SUPPLEMENT

"I COULDN'T PUT IT DOWN" TIME OUT

"The end is as unexpected as it is inevitable. The
book is translated from German, but the whole
thing is *tout à fait*" GUARDIAN

"This is definitely recommended for fans of Audrey Niffenegger and David
Nicholls. It really is a great read that will keep you hooked til the end!"
BOOK MONKEY SCRIBBLES

"This was a massive, million-plus bestseller in
Glattauer's native Germany, and it's easy to see why.
Short, striking and snappily written, it explores the
brilliant premise of love by accidental e-mail"
DAILY MIRROR

"A modern romance that feels both
fresh and traditional" SUNDAY TIMES

"Read it, you won't be disappointed" VULPES LIBRIS

DANIEL GLATTAUER was born in Vienna in 1960, where he works as a journalist and writer. Since 1989 he has been a columnist for *Der Standard*, and three collections of his articles have been published in book form. Both *Love Virtually* and *Every Seventh Wave* have been dramatised on Radio 4, starring David Tennant and Emilia Fox.

JAMIE BULLOCH (Leo) is the translator of novels by F.C. Delius, Martin Suter and Paulus Hochgatterer. KATHARINA BIELENBERG (Emmi) is an editor and translator. They are husband and wife.

EVERY SEVENTH WAVE

DANIEL GLATTAUER

Translated from the German by
Katharina Bielenberg and Jamie Bulloch

MACLEHOSE PRESS
QUERCUS·LONDON

First published in Great Britain in 2013 by

MacLehose Press
an imprint of Quercus
55 Baker Street
7th Floor, South Block
London WIU 8EW

First published in the German language as *Alle sieben Wellen*
Copyright © Deuticke im Paul Zsolnay Verlag Wien, 2009

English translation copyright © 2013 by
Katharina Bielenberg and Jamie Bulloch

The translation of this book is supported by the Austrian Federal
Ministry of Education, Arts amd Culture.

A CIP catalogue record for this book
is available from the British Library

ISBN 978 1 906694 98 2

This book is a work of fiction. Names, characters, businesses,
organizations, places and events are either the product of the author's
imagination or are used fictitiously. Any resemblance to actual
persons, living or dead, events or locales is entirely coincidental.

10 9 8 7 6 5 4 3 2 1

Designed and typeset in Apollo by Lindsay Nash
Printed and bound in Great Britain by Clays Ltd, St Ives plc

EVERY SEVENTH WAVE

CHAPTER ONE

Three weeks later

Subject: Hello

Hello.

Ten seconds later

Subject: Delivery Status Notification (Returned)

This is an automatically generated Delivery Status Notification

THIS E-MAIL ADDRESS HAS CHANGED. THE RECIPIENT CAN NO LONGER RECEIVE MAIL SENT TO THIS ADDRESS. ALL INCOMING MAIL WILL BE DELETED AUTOMATICALLY. FOR ANY QUERIES, PLEASE CONTACT THE SYSTEMS MANAGER.

Half a year later

Subject: (no subject)

Hello!

Ten seconds later

Subject: Delivery Status Notification (Returned)

This is an automatically generated Delivery Status Notification

THIS E-MAIL ADDRESS HAS CHANGED. THE RECIPIENT CAN NO LONGER RECEIVE MAIL SENT TO THIS ADDRESS. ALL INCOMING MAIL WILL BE DELETED AUTOMATICALLY. FOR ANY QUERIES, PLEASE CONTACT THE SYSTEMS MANAGER.

Thirty seconds later

Re:

Will this never stop?

Ten seconds later

Subject: Delivery Status Notification (Returned)

This is an automatically generated Delivery Status Notification

THIS E-MAIL ADDRESS HAS CHANGED. THE RECIPIENT CAN NO LONGER RECEIVE MAIL SENT TO THIS ADDRESS. ALL INCOMING MAIL WILL BE DELETED AUTOMATICALLY. FOR ANY QUERIES, PLEASE CONTACT THE SYSTEMS MANAGER.

Three days later

Subject: Query

Good evening, Mr Systems Manager. How are you? Quite chilly for March, don't you think? Still, after such a mild winter I don't think we should be complaining. Oh yes, since I'm here, I'd be grateful if you'd answer a query. We have an acquaintance in common. His name is Leo Leike. Unfortunately I appear to have mislaid his current e-mail address. Would you be so kind and possibly...? Many thanks.

With my warmest virtual wishes,
Emmi Rothner

Ten seconds later

Subject: Delivery Status Notification (Returned)

This is an automatically generated Delivery Status Notification

THIS E-MAIL ADDRESS HAS CHANGED. THE RECIPIENT CAN NO LONGER RECEIVE MAIL SENT TO THIS ADDRESS. ALL INCOMING MAIL WILL BE DELETED AUTOMATICALLY. FOR ANY QUERIES, PLEASE CONTACT THE SYSTEMS MANAGER.

Thirty seconds later

Re:

Do you mind if I give you some constructive criticism? You're being a tiny bit repetitive.

Enjoy your night shift,
Emmi Rothner

Ten seconds later

Subject: Delivery Status Notification (Returned)

This is an automatically generated Delivery Status Notification

THIS E-MAIL ADDRESS HAS CHANGED. THE RECIPIENT CAN NO LONGER RECEIVE MAIL SENT TO THIS ADDRESS. ALL INCOMING MAIL WILL BE DELETED AUTOMATICALLY. FOR ANY QUERIES, PLEASE CONTACT THE SYSTEMS MANAGER.

Four days later

Subject: Three questions

Dear Mr Systems Manager,

I'm going to be honest with you: this is an emergency. I need the current e-mail address of "User" Leo Leike, and I need it badly! I have three questions I urgently need to ask him: 1.) Is he alive? 2.) Is he still in Boston? 3.) Is he involved in an e-mail relationship with someone else? If the answer to 1.) is yes, I would forgive him 2.). But I could never forgive 3.). I don't mind if over the past half year he's tried to get it together again with Marlene fifteen times. I don't mind if

4

he's flown her in to Boston on a daily basis. I don't mind if
he's spent his nights hanging out in sleazy Boston plush
bars, and woken up every morning wedged between the
rock-hard breasts of some boring Barbie-blonde. I wouldn't
even mind if he'd pulled off three marriages and had three
sets of non-identical triplets. But there's one thing I would
mind: IF HE HAD FALLEN IN LOVE, BY E-MAIL, WITH
ANOTHER WOMAN HE HAD NEVER SET EYES ON.
Anything but that, please! That has to be a once-in-a-
lifetime thing. I need to be sure of this if I'm going to get
through these nights in one piece. The north wind is
blowing relentlessly.

Dear Mr Systems Manager, I think I can guess more or less
what your reply will be, but I'll ask you anyway: be a devil
and pass on my message to Leo Leike. I'm sure you're in
regular contact with him. Tell him it's about time he got in
touch. Do it! You'll feel better for it. O.K., now you can say
your piece again.

Best wishes,
Emmi Rothner

Ten seconds later

Subject: Delivery Status Notification (Returned)

This is an automatically generated Delivery Status
Notification

THIS E-MAIL ADDRESS HAS CHANGED. THE RECIPIENT
CAN NO LONGER RECEIVE MAIL SENT TO THIS
ADDRESS. ALL INCOMING MAIL WILL BE DELETED
AUTOMATICALLY. FOR ANY QUERIES, PLEASE CONTACT
THE SYSTEMS MANAGER.

Subject: Please forward

Hi Leo,

Are there new tenants in your flat? In case you're still in Boston, I thought I should warn you: don't be surprised if you get a massive electricity bill. They leave the lights on all night long.

Have a nice day – have a nice life,
Emmi

Two minutes later

Re:

Hello?

One minute later

Re:

Yoo-hoo, Mr Systems Manager, where are you?

One minute later

Re:

Should I be worried, or can I be hopeful?

Eleven hours later

Subject: Back from Boston

Dear Emmi,

Your intuition is uncanny. I've not been back in the country a week. As for the electricity, it's me using it. What I'd like to say, Emmi, is . . . what *would* I like to say after such a long time? Everything I might think of saying sounds pretty banal. The best I can come up with, even if it's five months early, is: Merry Christmas and a Happy New Year! I hope you're well, at least twice as well as I am.

Adieu, Leo.

One day later

Subject: Baffled

What was that? Was it anything? And if it was something, and whatever it was, was it the same thing as before? I don't believe it.

E.

Three days later

Subject: Stunned

Leo, Leo, what has happened to you? What has Boston turned you into?

E.

One day later

Subject: Closure

Dear Leo,

How you've made me feel over the past five days is worse
than you've ever made me feel, and you've made me feel
truly terrible before now. It was thanks to you that I
discovered for the first time quite how terrible terrible
feelings can be. (Good ones too, I should add.) But this one
is new to me: I've become a burden to you. You get back
from Boston, open Outlook, relishing the prospect of
reconquering your home country by e-mail. In pour the first
thrilling messages sent to you in error by female magazine
subscribers. Perfect fodder for fresh spiritual adventures
with anonymous women, and who knows, there might even
be an unmarried one among them. And then: Oh look, an e-
mail from someone called Emmi Rothner. The name seems
vaguely familiar. Wasn't she the one you practically wrote
into bed, like some kind of ace rat-catcher of the
cyberworld? You very nearly had her in your arms. But then
reason got the better of her at the last minute, and by a twist
of fate she never turned up, she let you down, so near and
yet so far. Nine and a half months pass, both the woman and
the frustration are long since forgotten. And then she gets in
touch, out of the blue she turns up in your inbox. And you
wish her – this is very funny, Leo, reminded me of you at
your best – a Merry Christmas and a Happy New Year, in the
middle of summer. And goodbye! She's had her chance.
Plenty more where she came from. She's in the way, she's
bugging me. So you're simply going to ignore me, Leo, is

that it? She'll give up eventually. She's already giving up. Well, she *will* give up, that's a promise!

Emmi

P.S. You say you hope I'm "at least twice as well" as you are. Unfortunately I don't know how well you are, Leo. Feeling twice as well as I do at the moment wouldn't amount to much, because I'm feeling at least ten times worse than I deserve to. But don't let it bother you.

P.P.S. Thanks for listening to me. Now you can send me your nice Systems Manager again. At least he and I could have a decent chat about the weather without being disturbed.

One hour later

Re:

I shouldn't have written back, dear Emmi. I've upset you (again), which I didn't mean to do. YOU COULD NEVER BE A BURDEN TO ME. You know that. Otherwise I'd have to be a burden to myself, because you're a part of me. I carry you around with me always, across all continents and emotional landscapes, as a fantasy, as an illusion of perfection, as the highest expression of love. That's how you existed for me for almost ten months in Boston, and that's how I brought you home with me.

But Emmi, in the meantime my physical existence has moved on; it had to move on. I'm in the middle of getting something started. I met someone in Boston. It's still too early to talk about . . . well, you know. But we want to make a go of it. She's thinking about taking a job here, she might move over.

That dreadful night, when our "first and last meeting" failed so miserably, I cruelly broke off our virtual relationship. You had come to a decision, even if you didn't want to admit it until the very end, and I helped you execute it. I don't know how things stand with Bernhard and your family at the moment. And I don't want to know, because it's got nothing to do with the two of us. I needed this long period of silence. (Maybe I should never have ended it.) We needed to protect the one-and-onlyness of our experience, to preserve for the rest of our lives our private, inner, intimate non-encounter. We took our relationship to the brink. It didn't get any further. It doesn't have a future, not even three quarters of a year down the line, particularly not now. Please see things the way I do, Emmi! Let's cherish what we had. And let's leave it at that, otherwise we'll ruin it.

Yours, Leo

Ten minutes later

Re:

That was a star performance, Leo, a real treat. You seem to be back on peak form already! – "You may well be the illusion of perfection, but I don't want to have anything more to do with you." I get it, I get it. More tomorrow. I can't let you off so lightly, sorry.

Goodnight

Your,
I. of .P

The following day

Subject: A fitting conclusion

O.K., I cherish what we had. And I'll leave it at that. I won't
ruin anything. I respect your position, my dear ex-e-mail
boyfriend Leo "It-couldn't-go-on" Leike. I'll content myself
with the fact that you want to retain lovely memories of me,
and of "our thing". To tell you the truth I feel rather
imperfect for an "illusion of perfection", and I'm massively
disillusioned, but I'm still your "highest expression of love",
even if I'm clearly from another planet. Because the thing
about Cindy – I bet she's called Cindy, I can just picture her
whispering "I'm Cindy" into your ear and giggling: "But
you can call me Cinderella", giggle, giggle – the thing with
Cindy is that you might not get the highest expression of
love, but you do get the physical side. You get it, and more
importantly you can live it. You carry me around with you
like some kind of "dream", as a natural balance between
body and spirit, and of course I completely understand that
you have to be careful that I don't become too heavy. You
don't want that dream to be shattered.

O.K. Leo, I'll make it easy for "us", I'll make it easy for you,
I'll make myself scarce, I'll stop, withdraw from your life. I
won't send you any more e-mails (soon!). I promise.

Do you mind if your "dream" asks for one last wish. One
very very very last wish? – I want ONE HOUR, one hour
face to face. There couldn't be a better way of preserving our
shared experience. The only sensible conclusion to our
intimate not-meeting would be a meeting. I won't demand
anything of you, I won't even expect anything of you. But I
have to see you at least once in my life. I have to speak to
you, and smell you. I have to watch your lips say the word

11

"Emmi" at least once. I have to have seen your eyelashes once, the way they bow down to me before the curtain falls.

You're right, dear Leo, there is no meaningful future for us. But there could be a fitting conclusion. That's all I'm asking of you!

Your Illusion of Perfection

Three hours later

Re:

Pamela.

One minute later

Re:

???

Thirty seconds later

Her name is not Cindy, it's Pamela. Yes, I know, it sounds pretty ghastly. It's always dangerous when fathers are allowed to choose their daughter's names. But she doesn't look at all like a Pamela, honest.

Goodnight, Emmi

Leo.

Forty seconds later

Re:

Dear Leo, I like you so much for that! Please forgive my sniping. I feel so, so, so weak.

Goodnight,
Emmi

CHAPTER TWO

The following day

Subject: Alright then

Let's meet.

Leo.

Three minutes later

Re:

One man, two word and a bit words! Excellent idea, Leo.
Where?

One hour later

Re:

In a café.

One minute later

Re:

With ten escape routes and five emergency exits.

Five minutes later

Re:

May I suggest Café Huber? We've never been as close anywhere else. (Physically, I mean.)

Forty seconds later

Re:

Are you going to send that nice sister of yours again, for a bit of Emmi-probing?

Fifty seconds later

Re:

No, this time I'll come straight up to you, alone and just as I am.

Three minutes later

Re:

I find your unfamiliar resolve rather irritating, Leo. Why, all of a sudden? Why do you want to meet me?

Forty seconds later

Re:

Because you want to.

Thirty seconds later

Re:

And because you want to get it over with.

Two minutes later

Re:

Because I want you to get over the idea that I want to get it over with.

Thirty seconds later

Re:

Stop being evasive, Leo. Admit you want to get it over with.

One minute later

Re:

Both of us want to get it over with. We want to get it out of the way once and for all. It's about giving it a "fitting conclusion". Your words, my dear Emmi.

Fifty seconds later

Re:

But I don't want you to meet me just so that you can get it over with. I'm not your dentist!

One and a half minutes later

Although you often hit right on a nerve. EMMI, PLEASE!!
We're going to go through with this now. It was your
explicit wish, and it was a reasonable wish. You made a
promise that it would not destroy our "us". I trust you and
your "us" and my "us" and our joint "us". We'll meet face
to face, for an hour, over a coffee. When are you free?
Saturday? Sunday? Lunchtime? Afternoon?

Three hours later

Subject: (no subject)

Am I not going to hear any more from you today, Emmi? If
not, goodnight! (If I am, goodnight!)

One minute later

Re:

Do you feel anything at all when you write to me, Leo?
Because I have the feeling you don't. And this feeling of
mine doesn't feel good at all.

Two minutes later

Re:

I have vast trunks and closets full of feelings for you, Emmi.
But I've also got the keys to lock them away.

Forty seconds later

Re:

Does your key come from Boston, by any chance, and is she called "Pamela"?

Fifty seconds later

Re:

No, it's a universal key and it goes by the name of "common sense".

Fifty seconds later

Re:

But your key only turns in one direction, it only closes things. And inside all those closets your feelings are beginning to suffocate.

Forty seconds later

Re:

My common sense makes sure that my feelings always get enough air.

Thirty seconds later

Re:

But they can't get out. They're never free. I'm telling you, Leo, you've got an entire warehouse of closeted feelings. You need to work on that. I'll say goodbye for today, then (my common sense is telling me to), and let the words you have or haven't spilled about our imminent meeting wash over me. Goodnight!

Twenty seconds later

Re:

Sleep well, Emmi.

The following day

Subject: Straight to the point

Hi Leo,

Let's get it over with, then: I can do Saturday at two. Shall I tell you what I look like, so you don't have to spend too long searching for me? Or would you rather I found you? You could be sitting somewhere in the crowd looking bored, leafing through a newspaper and waiting for me to come and talk to you. I could say something like: "Excuse me, is this seat taken? Erm, you wouldn't be Mr Leike, by any chance, the man with closeted feelings? Well, I'm Emmi Rothner, glad to meet you, or rather, to have met you at last. So..." – peering at the newspaper – "...what's going on in the world?"

Two hours later

Subject: Sorry

I'm really sorry about my last e-mail, Leo!! It was so, so, so...well, it wasn't particularly friendly, that's for sure. I probably deserve to get the Systems Manager for that one.

19

Ten minutes later

Re:

Which Systems Manager?

Fifty seconds later

Re:

Oh, don't worry about it. It's a running joke between me and myself. Does that work for you, Saturday at two?

One minute later

Re:

Two o'clock is fine. Have a good Wednesday, Emmi.

Forty seconds later

Re:

Which is more or less the same as saying: "That's the last e-mail you'll be getting from Leo today, Emmi."

Seven hours later

Subject: (No subject)

At least you're sticking to it!

Three hours later

Subject: Just for the hell of it

Is your light still on, Leo? (You don't have to reply. I was just wondering. And since I was wondering, I thought I might as well ask you.)

Three minutes later

Re:

Before you come up with the wrong answer yourself, Emmi, yes, my light is still on. Goodnight!

One minute later

Re:

So what are you up to? Goodnight.

Fifty seconds later

Re:

I'm writing. Goodnight.

Forty seconds later

Re:

Who are you writing to? Pamela? Goodnight.

Thirty seconds later

Re:

I'm writing to you. Goodnight.

Forty seconds later

Re:

To me? What are you writing? Goodnight.

Twenty seconds later

Re:

Goodnight.

Twenty seconds later

Re:

Oh, I get it. Goodnight.

The following day

Subject: Two days to go

Dear Leo,

This is the last e-mail I'm going to send you until you send me one (first). That's all I wanted to say, really. In case you don't reply, see you the day after tomorrow at Café Huber. I definitely won't be wandering through the café searching for you with a crazed look in my eye. I'll be sitting at a small table, somewhat apart from the crowd, waiting for the man who spent two years corresponding with me, building and dismantling feelings, until he decamped to Boston and locked away closets full of his own Emmi-feelings, waiting until this man finds me, so that we can bring this adventure of the mind to a fitting conclusion, once and for all. So I'm asking you to try your best to identify me. You have three versions to choose from, as you know. And in case you've forgotten your sister's descriptions, I'm happy to give you a few prompts. (It soooooo happens that I have your e-mail from back then.) Emmi One: petite, short dark hair (could have grown a fair amount in a year and a half, of course), boisterous, "a dignified arrogance masking a slight insecurity", a bit lofty, fine-featured, rapid movements, buzzing, temperamental. Emmi Two: tall, blonde, large breasts, feminine, a little slower in her movements. Emmi Three: medium height, brunette, shy, unsociable perhaps, melancholic. So I don't think you'll have any problem finding me. Do write back, and if you don't, have two relaxed/stress-free days. And take care of that key of yours!

Emmi

Ten minutes later

Re:

Dear Emmi, you've made it easier for me to recognize you, easier than you meant to, I expect. You've finally admitted that you're Emmi One, which is what I'd presumed all along. Do you want me to tell you why?

Re:

Damn right I do! I love it when the amateur psychologist in you gets all excited, Leo! It means I can resuscitate you when your heart stops beating and even force you to write e-mails when you're completely bottled up.

Fifteen minutes later

Re:

Dear Emmi One, it soooooo happens that I've also got our e-mails from back then, when we were practising telediagnosis on each other. For "Emmi Two", you glossed over my sister's observations about her being "self-confident, cool", the way she "looked at men very casually", and how she had "long, slim legs" and a "beautiful face". All that mattered to you was that she had slow movements and large breasts (something you've been shooting off about ever since we've known each other). It's obvious that you don't particularly like her. So you're not her. Same with "Emmi Three". She doesn't interest you. You dismiss her shyness immediately, this being in any case a trait which I suspect is alien to you. And you say nothing about her "exotic complexion", her "almond eyes", the way she avoided eye contact, all those things which might make her sound interesting. It's only with "Emmi One" that you're generous in your observations. You like to point out that her short, dark hair may have grown, you mention her "dignified arrogance masking a slight insecurity", and that she's a bit "lofty". You do say "buzzing", but you leave out "hectic" and "nervous". These are traits that you're not so happy about. So, my dear Emmi One, I'm looking forward to meeting you in the café on Saturday afternoon – dark hair, lofty and buzzing. See you soon, Leo.

Ten minutes later

Re:

If I'd known how euphoric you can be (can write) when you think you've seen through something, I'd have tried a little harder to be transparent, my love. I warn you, though, you should expect any one of those Emmis. Who knows what goes on in the outside world, and how strongly – or feebly – this is reflected here, where words make sense of themselves. Besides, of the two of us, you're the one who's been shooting off about large breasts. The very mention of them evidently triggers some kind of stressful oedipal situation. I don't know how else to describe it, but you always seem to be up on your "large breasts" high horse, if you'll forgive the metaphor.

Until soon,
Emmi

Five minutes later

Re:

That's something we can chat about in the café, if you like. It's looking as if we might not get beyond the subject of "breasts, yes, no, large, small", my dearest, my love, my dearest love.

Ten minutes later

Re:

Let's avoid the following discussion topics when we meet:

1.) Breasts and all other body parts. (I'd rather not talk about outward appearances – they'll be obvious enough.)

2.) "Pam" (and how she imagines her future in "Old Europe" with Leo Leike and his closets full of feelings).

3.) Plus all Leo Leike's other private matters that have nothing to do with Emmi.

4.) And all Emmi Rothner's private matters that have nothing to do with Leo Leike.

This hour should please, please, be about nothing other and no-one other than the two of us. Do you think we can manage that?

Eight minutes later

Re:

What are we going to talk about then? You haven't really left us with much.

Fifteen minutes later

Re:

You appear to be taking fright again, Leo – your chronic, dormant, contact-with-Emmi fear. You'd probably prefer to stick to "large breasts", am I right? I really don't mind what we talk about. Let's tell each other tales from our childhood. I won't pay any attention to the form and content of what you say, only to how you say it. I want to SEE you talk, Leo.

I want to SEE you listen. I want to SEE you breathe. After all this time of close, intimate, auspicious, measured, endless and yet curtailed, fulfilled and unfulfilled virtual reality, I'd just like to actually, finally set eyes on you. That's all.

Seven minutes later

Re:

I hope you're not going to be disappointed. Because I don't LOOK particularly exciting, neither when I'm talking, nor when I'm listening, and certainly not when I'm breathing. (I've got a cold.) But that's what you wanted; you were the one who wanted us to meet.

Three hours later

Subject: ??

Have I said something wrong (again)? Have a nice evening.

Leo

The following day

Subject: Scared

Good morning, Emmi. Yes, I'm scared. I'm scared that what I've meant to you (and maybe what I still mean to you) will evaporate the moment you set eyes on me. You see, I think that my on-screen words read better than my face looks when it utters them. You might be shocked when you discover who it is you've spent two years wasting all those words and feelings on, and what kind of feelings they were. That's what I meant when I wrote yesterday, "But that's what you wanted; you were the one who wanted to meet up." I hope you understand me now. If I don't get another reply from you, then see you tomorrow.

Leo

Five hours later

Re:

Yes, I do understand you now; you've made yourself beautifully clear. When it's been about "us", you've always talked exclusively about what you might mean to me, and in fact you still do. Because that's how you measure how much I might mean to you. In other words, if you mean a lot to me, I mean something to you. If you mean little to me, I mean nothing to you. My physical being is superfluous as far as you're concerned, and so you don't especially feel the need to meet me in person, which is why you're not exactly enthusiastic about being forced into it either. Because whoever and whatever I really am meant nothing and still means nothing to you. But back to your fear, perhaps I can put your mind at rest: What you mean to me is well on the way to evaporating, even before we meet (that's a poorly constructed sentence!). What you look like won't matter in the slightest, my dearest.

Ten minutes later

I think we'd best forget our meeting, my dearest.

Twenty seconds later

Re:

Yup, let's forget it. You might as well re-activate your out-of-office message, my dearest.

Ten minutes later

Re:

All my fault. I should never have replied to you after Boston.

One minute later

Re:

All my fault. I should never have written to say that lights were on in flat 15 at three in the morning. What has it got to do with me? Oh, by the way, in case you were getting what you mean to me out of all proportion, I just happened to be passing in a taxi.

Two minutes later

Re:

You're right, my lights have nothing to do with you, but I admit it was very kind of you to want to help me keep my electricity bill down. For the record — even if this is a meaningless comment now — you can't tell whether the lights are on in flat 15 from a taxi.

One minute later

Re:

O.K., so maybe it was a double-decker bus, or a propeller plane. From where we now stand it's irrelevant. Night night!

Seven hours later

Re:

In case you haven't just flown past, tonight the lights are on again in flat 15. I can't sleep.

Ten minutes later

Subject: Meaningful stuff

Let me get this clear, Emmi.

1.) What you mean to me means at least as much to me as what I mean to you.

2.) It's precisely because you *do* mean so much to me that it means a lot to me that I might also mean a lot to you.

3.) If you hadn't meant so much to me, it wouldn't have mattered to me how much I mean to you.

4.) But as it *does* really matter, this means that you mean so much to me that it has to matter how much I mean to you.

5.) If you knew how much you meant to me, you would understand why I don't want to stop meaning something to you.

6.) Conclusion one: You obviously had no idea how much you meant to me.

7.) Conclusion two: Maybe you do now.

8.) I'm tired. Goodnight.

Four hours later

Re:

Good morning, Leo. Nobody's ever said that to me. And I don't believe it's been said by anyone to anyone else before. Not only because no-one could ever formulate such a thing in such a (circuitous) way twice. But also because very few people can think with such intense feeling. I'm so very grateful for that. You have no idea what it means to me!!! See you later, 2 p.m. at Café Huber?

One hour later

Re:

2 p.m. at Café Huber.

One minute later

Re:

So that's four hours and twenty-six minutes.

One minute later

Re:

Twenty-five.

One minute later

Re:

Twenty-four.

Forty seconds later

Re:

And this time you're really going to be there!

Fifty seconds later

Re:

I certainly am. What about you?

Two minutes later

Re:

Of course. I'm not going to do us out of our "fitting conclusion".

Twenty minutes later

Re:

Was that your last e-mail, then?

Twenty seconds later

Re:

No. Was that yours?

Thirty seconds later

Re:

No, mine neither. Are you excited?

Twenty seconds later

Re:

Yes, I am. Are you?

Twenty-five seconds later

Re:

Very.

Thirty seconds later

Re:

You needn't be. I'm a pretty average person, nothing to get excited about when you first set eyes on me.

Twenty minutes later

Re:

It's far too late for damage limitation, Leo! So was *that* your last e-mail?

Thirty seconds later

Re:

My second last, dearest Emmi.

Forty seconds later

Re:

This one's my last! See you soon, Leo. Welcome to the World of Real-life Encounters.

CHAPTER THREE

That same evening
Subject: (no subject)
Thank you, Emmi.
Leo

The following morning
Subject: (no subject)
My pleasure, Leo.
Emmi

Twelve hours later
Subject: Was it...
...so awful?

Two hours later

Re:

Why do you ask? You know what it was like. You were there. You sat opposite your "illusion of perfection" in person for 67 minutes and smiled at her for at least 54 of them. I can't even begin to itemize everything you managed to pack into your smile, your range was that comprehensive. There was certainly a fair portion of embarrassment in amongst it all. But no, it wasn't awful. It wasn't awful at all. I hope your throat is feeling better. As I said: Isla mint lozenges, preferably redcurrant flavour. And gargle with sage tea before you go to bed!

Have a nice evening,
Emmi

Ten minutes later

Re:

"It wasn't awful at all." What was it then, dear Emmi? What was it *at all*?

Five minutes later

Re:

Hey Leo,

Since when have you been the one to ask all the exciting questions? Aren't you the one who's supposed to be providing the exciting answers? So if it wasn't awful, then what was it, Leo dear? Take your time.

Night night,
Emmi

Three minutes later

Re:

How can two identical Emmis write and speak in such
different voices?

Fifty seconds later

Re:

With a lot of training, Mr Language Psychologist! Now sleep
well, dream nice dreams and breathe freely.

By the way, dear Leo, your "Thank you, Emmi" was feeble.
Very feeble. Well below your potential.

The following evening

Subject: A stranger

Dear Emmi,

For an hour I've been deleting chunks of an e-mail in which
I'm trying to describe what I thought of you at our meeting.
I can't seem to collect my impressions. No matter what I
write about you, it sounds banal, clichéd, "well below my
potential". So now I'm going to try it the other way round.
I'll tell you what *you* thought of *me* when we met. I hope
you don't mind if I use one of your handy lists, just for a
change. O.K., here we go:

1.) You didn't like the fact that I got there before you.

2.) You were amazed that I recognized you straight away, because you knew that I hadn't counted on finding "this" Emmi.

3.) You were disconcerted when I kissed you on the cheek as if that had been something we'd been doing for years. (You didn't offer me the second cheek – I understood why.)

4.) Right from the word go you felt as though you were sitting with a stranger who claimed to be Leo Leike, but didn't offer any proof that he was the real Leo Leike.

5.) You didn't find this stranger at all disagreeable. He looked you in the eye. He made all the right noises at the right times. He didn't tell any rambling stories. He didn't panic when there were long gaps in the conversation. He didn't have bad breath, nor did his eyebrows twitch. He was entertaining and easy to be with, if a little hoarse. In spite of all this, you couldn't help enquiring of that beautiful, emerald-green watch, which had paired itself with the most delicate of wrists, how much longer you had to act out an intimacy – or have it acted out before you – which was wholly absent in that public arena. There was nothing about me you recognized. Nothing was familiar. Nothing touched you. Nothing reminded you of Leo the letter writer. Nothing from your inbox found its way to that table in the café. None of your expectations were fulfilled, dear Emmi. And that's why, as far as Leo Leike is concerned, you're somewhat . . . no, "disappointed" would be going too far. Disenchanted. Disenchanted is closer: "So that's really him, that's Leo Leike. O.K. I see." That's what you're probably thinking at the moment. Am I right?

One hour later

Re:

Yes, thanks for the compliment, Leo dear. My green watch is extremely beautiful, I've been wearing it for many years. I picked it up in Leipzig, at an antiques shop run by a Serb. "Runs well, you look in the day, you look in the night, always it shows the right time", that's what he promised me. And it's true: whenever I have looked at my watch, it has shown the right time. And it's showing the right time again now.

Lots of love,
Emmi

Ten minutes later

Re:

Dear Emmi,

What a terribly elegant way of dodging the issue, coquettish even! But don't you think it would be only fair if you told me why you're so pissed off? It would make life easier for me at night, sleeping and all that, if you get my drift.

Twenty minutes later

Re:

O.K. Leo, to tell the truth I would have been more interested to hear what *you* thought of *me*, and what *you* were feeling, or had felt (assuming you felt anything at all). I'm guessing I must know my own emotions and thoughts just a tiny bit better than you know them. Believe me. But sweet of you to go to all that trouble. Goodnight.

Subject: The man who wasn't there

Dear Leo,

I can tell that there's a slight tension in your communication at the moment. Perhaps you overdid it a bit, being so casual at the café. But I don't want to be a spoilsport: why don't I tell you how *you* felt when we met. Here goes:

1.) You were so well prepared to be Leo Leike the perfect, Leo Leike the smart, gallant, confident, yet modest bestower of fitting conclusions to e-mail relationships to any Emmi who happened to come your way, that it more or less didn't matter which Emmi it was.

2.) Congratulations, Leo, you barely let it show how dumbfounded you were that I looked so different from how you imagined.

3.) Congratulations again, you barely let it show how surprised you were that I could be of average height, brunette, shy and unsociable all at the same time. (For safety's sake, I left my melancholy in the cloakroom, and I'm glad I did.)

4.) And congratulations, Leo, you barely let it show how hard you found it to keep your crystal-clear eyes, the colour of a mountain stream, focused on mine, while maintaining your innocuous and reserved but friendly I'll-take-these-Emmis-as-they-come smile.

5.) In a top 100 of the most appealing blind dates which the average Emmi between the ages of 20 and 60 would opt to meet a second time – to go out stealing horses with, at least – you'd definitely rank in the top five. (You only get points deducted for that kiss on the cheek, which in its fleeting tilt at perfectionism was overhasty. You're going to have to fine-tune that.)

6.) But, alas, alas, alas! I'm not the average Emmi, I'm simply the one who thought she really knew you "personally", who knew you in those days (and nights!) when your closets of feelings were open wide. (And by the bye, your wine cabinet seemed to be open on most of those occasions too.)

7.) No, Leo dear, you weren't a stranger at all. You didn't even give me the chance to consider you a stranger. Because apart from an outer shell *you weren't there*; in public you concealed yourself from me.

8.) Our meeting synthesized into eight words: I was shy and you were closed up. Was that a disappointment? Well, if I'm going to be honest, yes, it was a little. The past two years – including the nine months you were in Boston, let's call it your inner Emmi-gration – certainly had a little more substance. Kiss on the cheek. I'm going to unpack my melancholy now, and take it with me into the shower.

Four hours later

Subject: One other thing

Nice jacket, by the way. Blue suits you. Oh, and have a good time in London! (No need to reply.)

Five minutes later

Re:

Do you mind if I ask you a "personal" question?

Fifty seconds later

Re:

This might be quite a question!

Forty seconds later

Re:

Are you and Bernhard still together?

Thirty seconds later

Re:

Of course. Yes, obviously. Definitely. Why do you ask?

Forty seconds later

Oh, you know, it's just a "personal" interest.

Twenty seconds later

Re:

In me?

Thirty seconds later

Re:

In your circumstances.

Fifty seconds later

Re:

Aha, I see. Can I ask you something "personal" too, Leo?

Twenty seconds later

Re:

You may.

Twenty seconds later

Re:

Do you regret having seen me?

Thirty seconds later

Re:

May I ask you another, deeply "personal" question?

Twenty seconds later

Re:

You may.

Thirty seconds later

Re:

Is it possible to regret it?

Forty seconds later

Re:

Should I answer that honestly and "very personally"?

Twenty seconds later

Re:

Yes, you should.

Thirty seconds later

Re:

I kept thinking: No, you can't regret it. But I could imagine you doing so.

Goodnight, my dear correspondent.

Twenty seconds later

Re:

Since I set eyes on you, my admiration for the confidence with which you're able to poke fun at your lack of confidence has risen tenfold. Goodnight, my dear correspondent.

Forty seconds later

Re:

That's nice, my virtual Leo is beginning to get the upper hand again. If you're thinking of giving your closets of feelings a little airing at some point, think of Emmi, the woman who pokes fun so confidently at her lack of confidence.

Thirty seconds later

Re:

Is "Pam" going to London with you?

Forty seconds later

Re:

She's already there.

Thirty seconds later

Re:

Oh, that's neat. Well, happy landings, and goodnight!

Twenty seconds later

Re:

Goodnight, Emmi.

CHAPTER FOUR

Four weeks later

Subject: Hello Emmi!

Hello Emmi,

Were you by any chance flying past flat 15 last night in your propeller plane, taking photos? Or was it just a storm? I was thinking of you in any case, and I couldn't get to sleep. How are you?

Love,
Leo

Five hours later

Re:

Hi Leo,

What a surprise! After the thorough post-mortem of our "encounter" and a month of silence I never thought you'd steel yourself to write me another e-mail. Who *are* you writing to, in fact? Who do you think of when you think of me (given that, charmingly, you were reminded of me by a thunderstorm)? Do you think of your faceless and bodyless "dream" of before, of your "highest expression of love", of your "illusion of perfection"? Or do you rather think of the shy girl from Café Huber who avoided eye contact? (If I hear from you within four weeks, I'll go one step further and ask you WHAT precisely you think of when you think of either of the above.)

Much love,
Emmi

Thirty minutes later

Re:

I'm thinking of the Emmi who, with fingertips so delicate they might vanish into the ether, brushes imaginary strands of hair from her face every thirty seconds and curls them behind her ears, as if she were trying to free her eyes from a veil, finally to see things as sharply and clearly as she has been describing them for ages. And I ask myself time and again whether this woman is truly happy in her life.

Ten minutes later

Re:

Dear Leo,

If I were to get an e-mail like that each day, I'd be the happiest woman in the world.

Three minutes later

Re:

Thank you, Emmi. But I'm sorry to say that happiness is not made of e-mails.

One minute later

Re:

Then what? What is happiness made of? Please tell me, I'm bursting to know!!!

Five minutes later

Re:

Out of security, trust, things in common, care, experiences, inspiration, ideas, beliefs, challenges, goals. And I'm sure this list is incomplete.

Three minutes later

Re:

Blimey! That sounds like a nightmare, like some kind of modern-day decathlon, entire weeks of activities around the theme of happiness, with an exhibition of its underlying virtues and features. I'd rather get a daily e-mail from Leo, with a small, imaginary lock of hair. Have a lovely evening! Glad you've not forgotten me.

Kiss on the cheek,
Emmi

The following day

Subject: A question

Dear Leo,

You know what I'm going to ask now!

Twenty minutes later

Re:

Your determined use of the exclamation mark gives me a
pretty good idea.

One minute later

Re:

So, what am I going to ask you then?

Three minutes later

Re:

"How was London?"

One minute later

Re:

Oh Leo, that might be how *you* would put it. But by now
you must know that I like to call things by their names. –
So: what's going on with "Pam"?

Fifty seconds later

Re:

First, "Pam" doesn't need inverted commas. Second, Pam is called Pamela. And third, Pam is not a thing.

Two minutes later

Re:

Do you love her?

Three hours later

Re:

It's taking you long enough to think about it.

Ten minutes later

Re:

It may be too soon to talk of that, Emmi, or even to discuss it.

Three minutes later

Re:

Nicely put, Leo. Now I have a choice. Either Leo means: it's too soon to call it love. Or he means: it's too soon to talk to Emmi about "Pam". Sorry, Pamela.

Five minutes later

Re:

Definitely the latter, Emmi. The way you've reverted so quickly to "Pam" tells me that you're not ready to talk about this. You don't like her, do you? You think she's taking your e-mail partner away from you. Am I right?

Five hours later

Subject: (no subject)

Now it's you who's taking your time, my love, trying to find a way to deny it.

Fifteen minutes later

Re:

O.K., you're right. I don't like her, first of all because I don't know her, so it's easier for me, secondly because I'm trying my best to imagine her in terms as unfavourable as possible, thirdly because I'm managing that quite successfully, and fourthly because, yes, she does take you away from me, the rest of you, the writing bit, the little bit of hope. Hope for...for...who knows what for? Just hope. But I promise you: if you *do* love her, then I'll learn to like her. Until then, do you mind if I say "Pam" a few more times? It makes me feel good, don't ask me why. And do you know what else makes me feel good, my love? When you write "my love". Because I take it literally. Yes, sometimes I manage that too. Sleep well.

Re:

You too, my love.

Subject: Me writing to you now

Emmmmmmmmmmmmmmmmi, I'm drunk. And I'm lonely. Big mistake. Never be both. Either lonely or drunk, but never both at the same time. Big mistake. You asked, "Do you love her?" Yes, I do love her when she's with me. Or to put it another way: I would love her if she were with me. But she isn't with me. And I can't be with her when she isn't with me. Do you understand, Emmi? I can't keep on loving women who aren't with me if I'm with them when I love them. London? How was London? Five days satisfying accumulated longing, six days of worrying about the longing yet to come. That's what London was like. Pamela wants to move over here to live with me. Call her "Pam", you can call her "Pam" if you like. Only you are allowed to do that. She wants to live with me. She wants to, but will she actually do it? I can't keep on living off the desires of a woman I love. Living *and* loving, both at the same time. Never one without the other. Drunk *or* lonely, never both at the same time. Always one without the other. Do you understand what I'm saying, Emmi?

Wait a second, I'm just going to pour myself another glass. Red wine, claret, the second bottle, tastes of Emmi, as ever. Do you remember? Did you know, Emmi, you're the only one? You're the only one, the only one, the only one, the . . . It's hard to find the right words. I'm a bit drunk already. You're the only one who's close to me even when you're not with me, because I'm still with you when you're not with me. And there's something else I've got to tell you, Emmi. No, I'm not going to, you have a family. You've got a husband who loves you. Back then you made a swift exit. You opted for him, you made the right decision. Maybe you're thinking you're missing something. But there's nothing missing from your life. Loving and living – you've got them both. I've got a both, too – I'm lonely and drunk. Big mistake.

But let me tell you something. I tried to force myself, tried so hard to force myself, I didn't want to like you. I didn't want it. I didn't want not to like you, and I didn't want to like you. I didn't want anything. I didn't want to see you. What was the point? You've got Bernhard and the children. And I've got Pamela. And when she's not with me, I've got claret. But let me tell you something else: You've got a gorgeous face, amongst other things. You look far more innocent than you write. No, you don't write as though you're guilty, but sometimes your words are so harsh, you take things to extremes. And yet your face is soft. And beautiful. And I don't know if you're happy. I don't know. I don't know. I don't know. But you must be. You can live and love, both at the same time. I'm lonely and I don't feel so great. And what do I get from Pamela if she's so far away that I stop feeling she's with me? Do you understand? I'm going to bed. But let me tell you something: I dreamt of you last night, and I saw your actual face. I don't care about your breasts, large breasts, small breasts, medium breasts, I don't care at all. But I *do* care about your eyes and your mouth. And your nose. The way you looked at me and talked to me, and your smell. I do care about all that. And now every word you write to me is your smell and your look, as well as your mouth. I'm going to bed now. I'll send this e-mail and then I'm going to bed. I hope I hit the right key. You're so close to me, I'm kissing you. And now I'm going to bed. Where's the key?

Five minutes later

Subject: I've written to you

Dear Emmi

I've sent you an e-mail. I hope you got it. No, I hope you didn't get it. Or, actually, yes. It doesn't matter, it is what it is, whether you read it or not. And now I'm going to bed. I'm a bit drunk.

The following evening

Subject: What a love!

Dear Leo

I got an e-mail from you yesterday evening. Do you remember? Did you re-read it today? Do you have it saved somewhere? If not, I can send it to you. You're such a love!!! You should get drunk more often. When you're drunk, you're so, so, so . . . "un-lonely". It feels like you're right here beside me.

One hour later

Re:

Thanks, Emmi. Early this morning, with a pounding head and an upset stomach, I discovered what I served up to you last night in my state of inebriation. And Emmi, "let me tell you something". Strangely, I'm not embarrassed by it. In some ways I'm even relieved. I wrote things that have been on my mind for a long time. I'm happy that they're now out in the open. And let me tell you something else – I'm happy that I've told *you* these things. I'm going to make myself a camomile tea now. Goodnight, my love. And please forgive me if I've gone too far.

The following morning

Subject: Second attempt

I want to see you again, Leo. For another coffee. Just a coffee in a café, that's all. Please say yes! We can make a better job of it than we did last time.

Have a nice day, my love.

Ten hours later

Subject: Café

Hi Leo,

Where are you? Not on your own again I hope, in some claret-induced coma. I just wanted to remind you of this morning's request: shall we meet again for coffee, yes or no? I'm going for "yes". How about you? If the votes are even, we'll go with the smaller shoe size. Would you be so kind as to share your vote with me today (even if you do happen to be sober)? I'd quite like to take the result to bed with me.

Kiss on the cheek,
Emmi
(the soft-faced one)

Two hours later

Subject: (no subject)

Leo, please write back!!!

One hour later

Subject: (no subject)

Oh Leo, do you have to? It drives me nuts, having to wait for answers to my pressing questions! Just write "yes", or "no", or even "bah!" – just write something, anything, but *write*! Otherwise a prop plane's going to land on the balcony of flat 15. You have been warned!

Emmi

The following morning

Subject: Harsh

Thanks, Leo. Thanks for an unforgettable night. I didn't sleep a wink.

Ten seconds later

Subject: Delivery Status Notification (Returned)

This is an automatically generated Delivery Status Notification

THIS E-MAIL ADDRESS HAS CHANGED. THE RECIPIENT CAN NO LONGER RECEIVE MAIL SENT TO THIS ADDRESS. ALL INCOMING MAIL WILL BE DELETED AUTOMATICALLY. FOR ANY QUERIES, PLEASE CONTACT THE SYSTEMS MANAGER.

Three minutes later

Re:

Leo, please tell me that you're just testing the limits with your attempts at tasteless jokes. If you get in touch right now, I may yet forgive you!

Emmi

Ten seconds later

Subject: Delivery Status Notification (Returned)

This is an automatically generated Delivery Status Notification

THIS E-MAIL ADDRESS HAS CHANGED. THE RECIPIENT CAN NO LONGER RECEIVE MAIL SENT TO THIS ADDRESS. ALL INCOMING MAIL WILL BE DELETED AUTOMATICALLY. FOR ANY QUERIES, PLEASE CONTACT THE SYSTEMS MANAGER.

One minute later

Re:

Why are you doing this to me?

Ten seconds later

Subject: Delivery Status Notification (Returned)

This is an automatically generated Delivery Status Notification

THIS E-MAIL ADDRESS HAS CHANGED. THE RECIPIENT CAN NO LONGER RECEIVE MAIL SENT TO THIS

ADDRESS. ALL INCOMING MAIL WILL BE DELETED
AUTOMATICALLY. FOR ANY QUERIES, PLEASE CONTACT
THE SYSTEMS MANAGER.

CHAPTER FIVE

The following evening

Subject: Test

Hello Emmi,

Let me know if you get this.

Leo

Half an hour later

Re:

Yes, I got it. But you get this, Leo, I haven't exactly enjoyed your company these past few days. What's the matter with you? Where have you been? What are you trying to do? What the hell are you playing at? Why are you setting the Systems Manager onto me? I thought for a moment that you'd run away back to Boston.

Re:

I'm sorry, Emmi. I'm really sorry! Evidently there's been a serious software error. My Outlook account was accidently unsubscribed. Maybe I missed a payment. I've had no messages for three days. Did you write to me?

Re:

Yes Leo, I did write to you. I asked you a question. I waited two and a half days for an answer. I was worried sick, felt like I did during those marvellous days before you escaped to America. I even tried to phone you. I wasn't going to say anything, I just wanted to hear your voice, but there was a message saying that your old number had "not been recognized". I wept at the thought of you, but no tears came. I giggled hysterically at the thought of you. It struck me that something which had never really begun was already over for a second time. Those were the high points of my miserable existence for the duration of your serious software error. As if there weren't enough things keeping us apart, the "system", which seems to have played a starring role in all this, throws another one into the mix. The space we're inhabiting is so creepy, I'm just shattered. Goodnight. Lovely to have you back. Lovely and comforting.

Three minutes later

Re:

Dear Emmi,

Please believe me, it pains me to have hurt you. It was an act of God: computer technology, whatever, separating us just as swiftly as it connects us. Our feelings are powerless against it. Forgive me. And sleep well, my love.

The following morning

Subject: Your question

Good morning, Emmi. I've just been on the phone to a "specialist". The "system" is up and running again. I hope you had a good sleep. Oh yes, you said you'd asked me something. What was it you wanted to know?

All my love,
Leo

One hour later

Re:

In short: today, 3 p.m., Café Huber?

Thirty minutes later

Re:

Yes, but (. . .). No, not but. Yes!

Twenty minutes later

Re:

Great! And it took you half an hour to come up with that remarkable causal chain, Leo dear? ONLY half an hour? Do you mind if I analyse it? First there was a "yes", an apparently resolute affirmative. Then came a comma, in expectation of an additional element to the sentence. Then there was a "but", heralding a qualification. After that came a round opening bracket. Then three points to convey a variety of thoughts shrouded in mystery. Then enough discipline to close the brackets and wrap up this confusing mystery. Then a traditional full stop to maintain the outward appearance of order and to mask inner turmoil. And then all of a sudden a truculent little "no", as if to signify a purposeful refusal. Another comma, anticipating additional information, and after that a "not", an outright rejection. And then another "but", a dissipation, a "but" that is only there to demonstrate that there isn't one any more. All doubt has been intimated. No doubt has been voiced. All doubt has been cast aside. And at the end what we're left with is a gutsy little "yes", complete with a defiant exclamation mark. To repeat: "Yes, but (. . .). No, not but. Yes!" What a poetic description of your fickleness. What a lyrical exposition of your decision-making processes. This man knows exactly that he doesn't know what he wants. And he knows better than anyone how to pass on this knowledge to the very individual it concerns. All in barely half an hour. Brilliant! And someone had the wit to sign you up for language psychology so that you could come up with *that*, Leo dear.

Three minutes later

Re:

Do you know what you want?

Thirty seconds later

Re:

Yes.

Forty seconds later

Re:

What?

Fifty seconds later

Re:

You. (For a coffee.) ((As you can see, even I have mastered the art of the bracket.))

Thirty seconds later

Re:

Why?

Re:

Because I'm doing the same thing as you, although it seems you can only admit it to yourself, open brackets, and me, close brackets, when you're drunk.

Forty seconds later

Re:

And what would that be?

Thirty seconds later

Re:

Being interested in you.

Forty seconds later

Re:

Yes, dear Emmi. No but, no full stop, no brackets. Just a plain and uncomplex "yes". Correct, well spotted. I am interested in you.

One minute later

Re:

Splendid, Leo dear. In that case I think all requirements for a second visit to the coffee house have been fulfilled. Three o'clock?

Twenty seconds later

Re:

Yes. Open brackets. Exclamation mark. Exclamation mark. Close brackets. Three o'clock.

CHAPTER SIX

Around midnight

Subject: You

Dear Leo,

This time I'll do the thanking (first). Thank you for this afternoon. Thank you for allowing me to peep through the narrow chinks into your closets full of feelings. What I saw has convinced me that you're the same person who writes to me. I recognized you, Leo. I recognized you again. You're the same person. You're one and the same. You're real. I like you very much! Sleep well.

Twenty minutes later

Re:

Dear Emmi,

There's a particular point on the palm of my left hand, roughly in the middle, where the life line is crossed by deep creases and turns down towards the artery. I look at it, but I can't see it. I stare at it but I can't pin it down. I can only feel it. I can feel it when I close my eyes, too. A point. It's such a strong feeling that it makes me dizzy. When I concentrate on it, I sense it extending through my body as far as my toes. It tingles, it tickles, it warms me, it churns my insides. It boosts my circulation, it governs my pulse, it determines the speed of my heartbeat. And in my head it intoxicates me like a drug, expanding my consciousness, broadening my horizons. A point. I could laugh with joy, because it makes me feel so good. I could weep tears of happiness, happiness at possessing it and being seized and filled by it to the very tips of my fingers.

Dear Emmi, in a certain café this afternoon – it must have been at around four o'clock – something happened on my left palm where this point is. My hand was reaching for a glass of water. The lissom fingers of another, softer hand came towards it; they tried to stop, tried to get out of the way, tried to avoid the collision. They almost succeeded. Almost. For a millisecond the soft tip of a finger breezing past rested on the palm of my hand as it reached for the glass. There was a delicate contact. I have stored it away. Nobody can take it from me. I can feel you. I recognize you. I recognize you again. You're the same person. You're one and the same. You are my point. Sleep well.

Ten minutes later

Re:

Leo!!! That was so lovely! Where do you learn stuff like that? Now I need a whisky. Don't let me bother you. Feel free to go to bed. And don't forget your point. I recommend you close your fist around it, to keep it safe.

Subject: Three whiskies and me

Dear Leo,

We stayed up a while and talked about you, the physical you. ("We" being me and three small whiskies.) It occurred to the first whisky and myself that when you're in my presence you're at pains to keep your words, gestures and expressions in check. The first whisky, who knew me quite well, said you didn't need to do this. (Unfortunately that one's long gone.) The second whisky, now also departed, suspected that you had decided ages ago to get no closer to me than you do in my inbox, or across a brightly lit café table under the protective gaze of a dozen witnesses. Given all this, today's conversation was pleasantly warm, affectionate, sincere, personal if not intimate, and it was even half an hour longer than we had planned. That's what the second whisky thought. There's a good chance that we could go on with this kind of Sunday-afternoon café meeting until we're pensioners, and play Patience together, or maybe a round of Tarock if our partners played too. (I'm sure "Pam" is a natural.)

Now, the third whisky, which can be a little fruity, asked about your physical feelings. (The whisky called it "libido", rather grandiloquently I thought. I told him that might be going a bit far.) He wanted to know whether I really believed that you only find me attractive with a blood-claret level of 3.8 parts per thousand. Because with coffee and water you seem to lack all interest in my physical appearance. I replied: "You're definitely wrong there, Whisky. Leo is a man who can concentrate all of his feelings, however strong, and whatever they are, into a single point in the middle of his palm. It wouldn't occur to a man like him to let a woman know if he found her attractive, and he certainly wouldn't say to her face: 'I like you!' He'd find that far too crude." And the third whisky said to me: "I bet he's said stuff like that to Pamela a thousand times." Do you know what I did with the third whisky after that, Leo dear? I annihilated it. And now I'm going to bed. Good morning!

Later that morning

Subject: Honestly, Emmi!

What was it you wrote the day after our first meeting? Let me quote: "'Thank you, Emmi' was feeble. Very feeble. Well below your potential."

And what did you say last night about our second meeting? Let me quote: "Because with coffee and water you seem to lack all interest in my physical appearance." That was feeble, Emmi. Very feeble. Well below your potential.

Three hours later

Re:

Leo, I'm sorry. You're right, that sentence sounded ridiculous. If you'd written it, I'd have laid into you. The whole e-mail is embarrassing. Vain. Touchy. Smarmy. Bitchy. Yuck! But you've got to believe me: IT WASN'T ME, IT WAS THE THREE WHISKIES! I've got a headache. I'm going to go and lie down. Bye bye!

The following evening

Emmi, I'm sorry. I need to try to re-evaluate what you've said (and your whiskies have said). So I'm going to ask you, in all seriousness and without a trace of humour, as befits my personality: Why should I have any "interest in your physical appearance"? Why should I say to your face, "I like you"? Why should I get any closer to you than across the table of a well-lit café? Surely you don't want me to fall in love with you "physically", too (or libidinously, as the booze puts it)?! Where would that get you? I don't understand, you'll have to explain. In fact, there are a number of things that need an explanation, my dear. Over coffee you managed yet again to be elegantly evasive. You've been skirting around the issue for months – since Boston, in fact. But now I want to know. Yes, I really do want to know. Exclamation mark, exclamation mark, exclamation mark, exclamation mark.

Here's my first questionnaire: How's your relationship? How are things with you and Bernhard? What are the children up to? What goes on in your life? Questionnaire two: Why did you resume contact with me after Boston? What do you now think about the circumstances that led to the break in our correspondence? How could you forgive Bernhard? How could you forgive me? Questionnaire three: What is missing from your life? What can I do for you? What do you want to do with me? What should I be for you? How should we go on from here? Should we go on at all? And where to? Please tell me: WHERE TO? Give yourself a few days before you answer; time is the one thing we have in abundance.

Have a nice evening,
Leo.

Five hours later

Subject: Impressions

Just want to add a few words to my non-existent or indiscernible "interest in your physical appearance", dear Emmi. Please tell your former and future whiskies that I like you. I can say that with 0.0 parts per thousand of alcohol in my blood. It's lovely to look at you. You're stunning to look at. And fortunately I can look at you any time I choose. Not only have I got hundreds of impressions of you, I also have an impression *from* you. I have a point of contact on my palm. I can look at you there. I can even caress you. Goodnight.

Three minutes later

Re:

You've just answered the question "What can I do for you?" yourself. Caress the point of contact, my love.

One minute later

Re:

I will. But I'll do it for me, not for you. Because only I can feel this point, it belongs to me, my love!

Fifty seconds later

Re:

That is a misapprehension, my love! A point of contact always belongs to two people. 1.) The contacter. 2.) The contactee.

Goodnight.

71

Three days later

Subject: Questionnaire one

Fiona is about to turn eighteen. She finishes school next year. At the moment I'm only speaking to her in English or French, so she can practise. Which means she's not speaking to me at all any more. She wants to be an air hostess or a concert pianist. I'm trying to persuade her that she can do both: an in-flight pianist, a flying piano player. There'd be no competition. She's pretty, slim, medium height, blonde, fair skin, freckles – just like her mother. She's been "going out" with Gregor for the past six months. "Going out with Gregor" seems to be code for staying up all night with anyone, male or female. Officially she spends every night with him. The poor guy doesn't seem to be aware of this, much less does he get anything out of it. "What do you two spend the whole time doing?" I ask. She smiles at me as wickedly as she can. Hinting at "sex" is still the best strategy for uncommunicative teenagers. It's obvious. No need for Fiona to waste her breath. She'll just have to put up with a few lectures on contraception and safe sex.

Jonas is fourteen, and still a child. He's sensitive and quite clingy. He misses his mother, and he needs me very much. He keeps the family tightly together, and it's a major effort for him. He has no energy for school. Every few days he asks whether I still love his father, and Leo, you can't imagine how he looks at me. For him the nicest thing in the world is to see us both happy, and he's the main focus for both of us. Sometimes he even pushes me into his father's arms. He tries to force the two of us together, to make us more intimate. He can sense that little by little this intimacy is slipping away from us.

Bernhard, yes, Bernhard! What can I say, Leo? And why should I have to say it to you, of all people? I'm finding it hard enough to admit it to myself. Our relationship has cooled. It's no longer an affair of the heart, but merely a kind of mental exercise. I have nothing to reproach him for, unfortunately. He never displays any weaknesses. He's the kindest, most unselfish person I know. I like him. I respect his decency. I cherish his attentiveness. I marvel at his calm, and his intelligence.

But no, it's no longer the "great love" it once was. Perhaps it *never* was. But we so enjoyed our staging of it, and acting out our parts to each other, playing them to the children so that they could feel secure. But after twelve years of shifting the scenes we've tired of our roles as partners in a perfect marriage. Bernhard is a musician. He loves harmony. He needs harmony. He lives it. WE live it together. I decided to be a part of this whole. If I withdraw, I would bring about the collapse of everything we've built for ourselves. Bernhard and the children have already lived through one collapse. There cannot be another. I couldn't do that to them. I couldn't do it to myself. I would never forgive myself. Do you understand?

One day later

Subject: Leo?

Hello, my love, have you lost your tongue? Or are you waiting patiently for parts two and three of my family saga?

Five minutes later

Re:

Do you talk to him about it, Emmi?

Six minutes later

Re:

No, we make a point of not talking about it. It seems to work better that way. We both know only too well what it's all about. We try to make the best of it. You must not think that I'm desperately unhappy, Leo. This corset I wear is a good friend; it supports and protects me. I just have to be careful that one day it doesn't take my breath away altogether.

Three minutes later

Re:

Emmi, you're thirty-five!

Five minutes later

Re:

Thirty-five and a half. And Bernhard is forty-nine. Fiona is seventeen. Jonas is fourteen. Leo Leike is thirty-seven. Mrs Kramer's bulldog Hector is nine. And what about Vasilyev, the Wiessenbachers' little terrapin? Remind me to ask them, Leo! But what are you trying to say? At thirty-five am I not old enough to be logical? At thirty-five am I not old enough to take responsibility? Am I not old enough to know what I owe to myself and to my life, and what I have to be resigned to in order to remain true to myself?

Re:

Whatever, you're far too young to start worrying that your corset might take your breath away altogether, my love.

One minute later

Re:

As long as Leo Leike is around to worry about my air supply, via e-mail or sometimes even in real life at a café table, I don't think I'll get into breathing difficulties.

Two minutes later

Re:

Nice try at changing the subject, Emmi dear. May I remind you that many of my questions remain unanswered? Are they saved, or should I send them again?

Three minutes later

Re:

I've saved everything you've ever written to me, my love. Enough for today. Have a nice evening. You're a good listener, Leo. Thank you.

The following day

Subject: Questionnaire number three

I'm saving your second questionnaire, the weird one, until last. I'd rather leap straight into the present.

What is missing from my life, Leo? – You. (Even before I knew that you existed.)

What can you do for me, Leo? – Just be there. Write to me. Read me. Think of me. Stroke your palm where I touched you.

What do I want to do with you, Leo? – Depends on the time of day. Mostly I want to have you in my head. Sometimes below it.

What should you be for me, Leo? – The question is superfluous. You already are.

How will this go on, Leo? – The same as before.

Should it go on? – Definitely.

But where will it go? – Nowhere. Just on. You live your life, I live mine. And the rest we'll live together.

Ten minutes later

Re:

That won't leave very much for "us", my love.

Three minutes later

Re:

That depends on you, my love. My reserves are deep.

Two minutes later

Re:

Un(ful)filled reserves. I won't be able to fill them, my love.

Fifty seconds later

Re:

You can have no idea what you can fill, my love, what you can fill and what you have already filled. Don't forget that you have vast closets of feelings at your disposal. You just need to give them an airing once in a while.

Fifteen minutes later

Re:

I just want to know one thing: Have our two encounters changed anything for you?

Forty seconds later

Re:

Have they for you?

Thirty seconds later

Re:

Your turn first: For you?

Twenty seconds later

Re:

No, you first: Has anything changed for you?

One minute later

Re:

O.K., I'll go first. But before that you have to answer my outstanding questions. That's only fair, my love.

Four hours later

Subject: Questionnaire number two

O.K., let's get this over with:

1.) Why did I get in contact with you again after Boston? Why indeed? – Because the nine months that were "Boston" were the worst nine months ever since years have been divided into months. Because the man of many words slipped wordlessly out of my life. Spinelessly through a back door in the outbox, which was bolted shut with one of the very worst messages in the history of modern communication. That sentence is still the stuff of my nightmares (and if technology is feeling malicious, it's sometimes the stuff of my inbox too – Delivery Status Communication (Returned), bla bla bla).

Our "story" was never concluded, Leo. Flight is never an ending in itself, it merely postpones the end. You know that very well. If you didn't, you wouldn't have written back to me, nine and a half months later.

2.) What do I now think about the circumstances that led to the break in our correspondence? – What kind of question is that? The whole thing had got too much for you, too much or too little. Too little for all your emotional investment, your outlay on illusions. Too much for practical gains, for tangible revenue. Emmi plc was no longer profitable. You lost patience with me. Those, Leo dear, were the circumstances that led to the break in our correspondence.

3.) This is where it gets exciting. How could I forgive Bernhard? I've read this question at least twenty times, but I don't understand it, I really don't. WHAT could I possibly have had to forgive Bernhard for? The fact that he's my husband? That he stood in the way of our e-mail love affair? The fact that, in the end, his very existence was responsible for your flight? What are you trying to get at, Leo? You'll have to explain it to me.

4.) In conclusion: How could I forgive you? Oh, Leo. I'm easily corruptible. A few nice e-mails from you and I can forgive you everything, even a dramatic pause that went on for nine and a half months. That's it!!!

Ten minutes later

Subject: (no subject)

So, my love, now you're going to tell me whether anything has changed as a result of our meeting. (And if so, what, of course.)

A kiss on the cheek and a stroke of the palm on the special point,
Emmi

CHAPTER SEVEN

The following evening

Subject: Leo?

Leo?

The next morning

Subject: Wake-up call

Leo?

Leeeooo?

Leo eo eo eo eo eo eeeeeooooooooo??

Le e e e e e e e e e eeeeeeeeeeeeeeeeeeeooooooooo??

Eleven hours later

Subject: Meeting

Dear Emmi,

Could we have another meeting? There's something I've got to tell you. I think it's important.

Ten minutes later

Re:

"Pam"'s pregnant!

Three minutes later

Re:

No, Pamela is not pregnant. It's got nothing to do with Pamela.

Can you spare a few minutes tomorrow or the day after?

One minute later

Re:

Sounds very dramatic! If it's good news that is so urgent all of a sudden and has to be relayed in person, then yes, I can "spare a few minutes"!

Two minutes later

Re:

It's not good news.

Forty seconds later

Re:

Then give it to me in writing. Today, please! Tomorrow will be a tough day. I need at least a few hours' sleep.

Ten minutes later

Re:

Please, Emmi, let's discuss this in peace sometime over the next few days! Now go to bed, and don't lose sleep over it. O.K.?

Forty seconds later

Re:

I'm always happy to be comforted, Leo, but I won't be fobbed off. Not by you. Not like this. Not with the words "go to bed and don't lose sleep over it". So come on, tell me.

Thirty seconds later

Re:

Believe me, Emmi, this subject has no place in your goodnight inbox. We need to talk about it face to face. A few days won't make any difference.

Fifty seconds later

Re:

LLL, TTT!!!!

(Listen, Leo Leike, tell the truth!!!!)

Ten minutes later

Re:

O.K., Emmi. Bernhard knows about us. Or at least he did
know about us. That's why I bowed out.

One minute later

Re:

??? What kind of absurd statement is that, Leo? What is it
that Bernhard knows? What was there to know? And how
do *you* know? If anyone was going to know, it would be me,
don't you think? You seem to have got carried away by some
weird conspiracy theory. I demand an explanation!

Three minutes later

Emmi, ask Bernhard, please! PLEASE TALK TO HIM! It's up
to him to explain all this, not me. How was I to know that he
never told you? It's unimaginable. I refused to believe it. I
simply thought you didn't want to talk to me about it. But it
seems as if you really don't know. He hasn't told you, even
to this day.

Two minutes later

Re:

I'm beginning to worry about you. Have you got a fever?
Where are your fantasies leading you? Why in God's name
should I talk to Bernhard about you? What do you imagine
that I would tell him? "Bernhard, we've got to talk. Leo
Leike says you know all about him, or rather about us. Who

is Leo Leike? You don't know him. He's the man I've never set eyes on, and haven't told you about either. So you can't possibly know him. But now he insists that you do know about him, and about us . . ."

Come on, Leo, get a grip. You're making me nervous!

One minute later

Re:

He read our e-mails. And afterwards he sent me an e-mail himself. He asked me to meet you once and then leave you in peace. After that I took the job in Boston. That's it in a nutshell. I'd rather have told you this face to face.

Three minutes later

Re:

No. I don't believe that. That's not Bernhard. He would never do that. Tell me it's not true. It can't be true. You have no idea of the harm you're doing. You're lying to me. You're destroying everything. That's a monstrous thing to say about anyone, and Bernhard does not deserve it. Why are you doing this? Why are you wrecking everything between us? Or are you bluffing? Is that supposed to be a joke? What kind of a joke do you call that?

Two minutes later

Re:

Dear Emmi,

I can't rewrite the past now. I hate myself for it, but there were only two options open to me. Either bow out and keep quiet about it forever. Or the truth. Much too late. Unforgivably late. Unforgivable, I know. I'm attaching the e-mail Bernhard sent over a year ago, on 17 June, immediately after his "collapse" on that hiking holiday with the children in the South Tyrol.

Subject: To Mr Leike

Dear Mr Leike,

I have found it very hard to write you this message. I'll admit I'm embarrassed, and the embarrassment I'm bringing upon myself increases with every line. My name is Bernhard Rothner – I believe I don't need to give you more of an introduction. Mr Leike, I have a huge favour to ask of you.

When I tell you what this favour is you will be amazed, possibly even shocked. I will then try to explain my motives for asking this favour. I am no great writer, regrettably, and I'm not really familiar with e-mail. But I will endeavour to say all those things that have been concerning me for months, things which have put my life out of joint, my life and that of my family, even my wife's, and I believe I can judge this accurately after so many harmonious years of marriage.

And so to the favour: Mr Leike, meet my wife! Please do it, finally, and bring this nightmare to an end! We're grown men, I can't dictate what you do. I can only implore you:

85

meet her! I'm feeling inferior and powerless, and suffering because of it. How humiliating do you think it is for me to write such lines as these? You, on the other hand, haven't shown the slightest weakness, Mr Leike. You have nothing to reproach yourself for. And me, I don't have anything to reproach you for either, unfortunately. I really don't. You can't reproach a mind. You're not palpable, Mr Leike, you're not tangible. You're not real. You're just my wife's fantasy, an illusion of unlimited emotional happiness, an other-worldly rapture, a utopia of love, but all fashioned out of words. Against this I'm impotent; all I can do is wait until fate is merciful and turns you at last into a creature of flesh and blood, a man with contours, with strengths and weaknesses, something to aim at. Only when my wife can see you as she sees me, as someone vulnerable, an imperfect being, an example of that flawed construct which is man; only when you have met face to face will your superiority vanish. Only then can I compete with you on an equal footing, Mr Leike. Only then can I fight for Emma. My wife once wrote to you, "Leo, please don't force me to open my family album." But now I find myself obliged to do it in her stead. When we met, Emma was twenty-three and I was her piano teacher at the Academy of Music, fourteen years her senior, happily married and the father of two delightful children. A car accident destroyed our family – our three-year-old was traumatized, the elder one badly injured. I suffered permanent injuries, and the children's mother, my wife Johanna, died. Without the piano I would have fallen apart. But music when it's played is life itself – nothing can remain dead for ever. If you're a musician and you play music, you live out memories as if they were happening now. Music helped me pull myself back together. And then there were my pupils, there was a distraction, there was a job to do, there was meaning. And then, out of the blue, there was Emma. This lively, sparkling, sassy, gorgeous young woman began – all by herself – to pick up the pieces of our life, without expecting anything in return. Extraordinary people like her are put on to this earth to counter sadness. They are few and far between. I don't know how I deserved it, but suddenly she was there by my side. The children ran straight to her, and I fell head over heels in love with her.

What about her? Mr Leike, I bet you're wondering, "But what about Emma?" Did she, this 23-year-old student, fall equally in love with this sorrowful old knight, soon to be forty, who was being kept together by little more than keys and notes? I can't answer this question, not to you, nor even to myself. How much was it down to her admiration for my music? (I was very successful at the time, an acclaimed pianist.) How much was pity, sympathy, a desire to help, the capacity to be there through the bad times? How much did I remind her of her father, who left her when she was very young? How much of it was her doting on my sweet Fiona and little, golden Jonas? To what extent was it my own euphoria reflected in her, to what extent did she love my boundless love for her, rather than love me? How much did she relish the certainty that I would never be unfaithful, a guaranteed lifetime of dependability, the assurance of my eternal loyalty? Please believe me, Mr Leike, I would never have dared get close to her if I had not felt that her feelings for me were as strong as mine for her. It was obvious that she felt drawn to me and the children; she wanted to be part of our world, an influential part, a definitive part, the heart of it. Two years later we got married. That was eight years ago. (I'm sorry, I've just ruined your game of hide-and-seek:

the "Emmi" you know is thirty-four years young.) Not a day passed without my astonishment at having this vital young beauty at my side. And every day I waited in trepidation for "it" to happen, for a younger man to appear, one of the many who have admired and idolized her. And Emma would say, "Bernhard, I've fallen in love with somebody else. Where do we go from here?" This nightmare has failed to materialize. A far worse one has come to pass. You, Mr Leike, the silent "other world". Illusions of love via e-mail, feelings intensifying day by day, a growing yearning, unsated passion, everything directed towards one apparently real goal, an ultimate goal which is forever being postponed, the meeting of all meetings, but one which will never take place because it would dispel the artifice of ultimate happiness, total satisfaction, without end, with no expiry date, which can be lived only in the mind. Against that I'm impotent.

Mr Leike, since you "arrived", as it were, it's as though Emmi is transformed. She's absent-minded and distanced from me. She sits in her room for hours on end, staring at the computer screen, into the cosmos of her dreams. She lives in her "other world", she lives with it. When there's a beatific smile on her face, it's no longer for me – it hasn't been for a long time. She has to make a real effort to hide her distraction from the children. I can see just what a torture it is for her to sit next to me now. Do you know how much that hurts? I've tried to ride out this phase by being extremely tolerant. I've never wanted Emma to feel constrained by me. Neither of us has ever been jealous. But all of a sudden I no longer knew what to do. I mean, there was nothing and nobody there, no actual person, no obvious interloper – until I discovered the root of the problem.

I could have died with shame that the whole thing had gone as far as it has. I snooped around in Emma's room. Eventually, in a secret drawer, I found a folder, a fat folder full of documents: her entire e-mail correspondence with a certain Leo Leike, printed out nice and crisp, page by page, message by message. I copied these documents with a trembling hand, and for a few weeks I managed to put them out of my mind. We had a ghastly holiday in Portugal. The little one was ill, the older one fell madly in love with a sports instructor. My wife and I didn't say a word to each other for a fortnight, but both of us tried to fool the other that everything was just fine, as it always was, as it always had to be. After that I could hold out no longer. I took the folder with me on the walking holiday, and in a fit of self-destruction, out of some masochistic desire to make myself suffer, I read through all the e-mails in one night. Let me tell you, since the death of my first wife I have experienced no greater emotional torture. When I had finished reading I couldn't get out of bed. My daughter phoned the emergency services and I was taken to hospital. My wife collected me the day before yesterday. Now you know the whole story.

Mr Leike, please meet Emma! And now I come to the wretched nadir of my self-humiliation. Meet her, spend a night with her, have sex with her! I know that you'll want to. I'll "allow" you to. I'm giving you *carte blanche*, I'm absolving you of all scruples, I won't think of it as infidelity. I sense that Emma wants physical as well as mental intimacy with you, she wants to "know" it, thinks she needs it, something's urging her to do it. That's the thrill, the novelty, the variety I cannot offer her. So many men have worshipped and lusted after Emma, but it never struck me that she felt attracted to any of them. And then I saw the e-mails she has written to you. Suddenly I understood just how great her desire can be if aroused by the "right one". You, Mr Leike, are her chosen one. And I'm almost wishing you would sleep with her once. ONCE (like my wife I'm using emphatic block capitals). ONCE. JUST ONCE! Let that be the culmination of the passion you have built up in writing. Make that the conclusion. Crown your e-mail correspondence, and put a stop to it. Give me back my wife, you unearthly, untouchable being! Release her. Bring her back down to earth. Let our family continue to live. Don't do it as a favour to me or my children. Do it for Emma, for her sake. I beg you!

And now I come to the end of my embarrassing, distressing *cri de coeur*, my excruciating appeal for mercy. Just one final request, Mr Leike. Don't betray my confidence. Leave me outside your shared narrative. I have abused Emma's trust, I have gone behind her back, I have read her private, intimate correspondence. I have atoned for this. I could never look her in the eye again if she knew I had been spying. She could never look me in the eye again if she knew what I had read. She would hate both herself and me in equal measure. Please, Mr Leike, spare us that. Don't tell her about this letter. Once more, I beg you!

So now I'm going to send the most excruciating letter I have ever written.

Yours sincerely,
Bernhard Rothner

CHAPTER EIGHT

Three days later

Subject: Emmi?

Emmi?

(I'm not expecting an answer. I just want you to know that I'm asking the question every single second.)

Two days later

Subject: (no subject)

Maybe you despise me for every sentence I've ever written to you. Maybe you hate me for every word I'm sending now. But what else can I do? How are you, Emmi? I'd love to be there for you. I'd love to be able to do something meaningful for you. I'd love to know what you're thinking and feeling. I'd love to think and feel with you. I'd love to shoulder half of your burdens, however unpleasant they may be.

Two days later

Subject: (no subject)

Should I not write to you any more?

The following day

Subject: (no subject)

What does this mean, Emmi? Does it mean:

You don't even know yourself whether you want me to write to you.

You don't care whether I write to you or not.

You're absolutely sure you don't want me to write to you.

You're not reading my e-mails any more.

Three days later

Subject: The north wind

O.K., Emmi. I get it, I won't write any more.

If . . . the north wind . . . you know . . . always.

Always, always, always, always, always!

All my love,
your Leo.

Five hours later

Re:

Hi Leo,

Are you asleep?

Three minutes later

Re:

EMMI!!! THANK YOU!!!

How are you? Please tell me! I can't think about anything
else. I ought to be finishing off a research report, but I've
been sitting in front of the screen for hours, staring at the
toolbar with the envelope icon and waiting for a four-letter
miracle. It's here. I can't believe it. EMMI. You're back!

Thirty seconds later

Re:

Can I come and see you?

One minute later

Re:

I beg your pardon, Emmi? Did I read that right? You want to
come to my place? To my home? Flat 15? Why? When?

Twenty seconds later

Re:

Now.

Fifty seconds later

Re:

Dear Emmi,

Are you serious? Are you feeling O.K.? Do you need to talk? Of course you can come over. But it's two o'clock in the morning. Wouldn't it be better if we met up tomorrow? We'd have more time, and clearer heads. (I would, at least.)

Twenty seconds later

Re:

Can I come over, yes or no?

One minute later

Re:

It sounds a little threatening, but yes, of course you can, Emmi.

Thirty seconds later

Re:

Do you have any whisky, or do I have to bring my own?

Forty seconds later

Re:

I've got whisky. The bottle is three-quarters full. Is that enough for you? Emmi, you couldn't by any chance let me know what mood you're in, could you? Just so I can prepare myself.

Twenty seconds later

Re:

You'll find out soon enough. See you soon!

Forty seconds later

Re:

See you soon!

The following evening

Subject: Nadir

Dear Emmi,

I don't imagine you're feeling any better today, neither better than yesterday, nor better than me. Furiously heaping some of the damage onto the person who might have caused it in the first place doesn't automatically make you feel any less wounded. Paying someone back simply means that you're poorer afterwards. Your tempestuous entrance, the denial of your shyness, the abandonment of your fear, your "exhilarating demand", which I would not – and you knew this very well – have wanted to or been able to turn down, your perfectly executed plan, taking things to their limit and then letting it all go, as if intimacy were the most worthless thing on earth; your calculated departure, your skilful disappearance – none of this was retaliation, but an act of desperation. The looks you gave me afterwards seemed to say, "Isn't that what you wanted from the very start? Well, now you've had it." No, it's not what I wanted at all, and you know it! We have never been so close and yet so far apart. That was our nadir. You can't fool me, Emmi. You're not the cool, powerful, self-assured woman who can turn humiliation into victory like that.

The only punishment I really felt was your silence. What has connected us and bound us together until now has been words. If you have any feelings left for me at all, then talk to me!

Leo

Three hours later

Re:

So you want words. Fine, my mouth is full of them and I'll give them to you gladly, what else can I do with them.

You're right, Leo. I wanted to prove it to Bernhard. I wanted to prove it to you. And to myself. Now I know that I'm capable of cheating. What's more, I can cheat on Bernhard. What's more, I can cheat on Bernhard with you. What's more – my greatest achievement – I can cheat on myself at the same time. Thanks for "playing along", by the way. I know it had nothing to do with an inability to control your urges – it was pure compassion. You offered to deal with half my feelings. Considering the strained circumstances, you coped with this brilliantly yesterday morning. A bed shared means half a bed. Suffering shared means double the suffering.

You're right, Leo. I don't feel any better today. In fact I feel shittier than ever.

You cannot imagine, Leo, what "you two" have done to me. I feel betrayed, sold down the river. My husband and my virtual lover made a pact behind my back: if the one wants to feel me physically, just once, the other will make an exception, turn a blind eye. If the one then disappears, never to be seen again, the other can keep me forever.

The one gives me back to my husband, the rightful owner, as if I had been a find. In return, the other allows me a "physical encounter" – a sexual adventure with an otherwise virtual fantasy love-figure, like some kind of finder's reward. A scrupulous division, a perfect separation, a perfidious conspiracy. And daft little Emmi, bound to her family and yet driven by a thirst for adventure, won't ever hear a word about it. Oh yes.

I cannot even begin to gauge what this might mean for Bernhard and myself, Leo. And you will probably never know. As for what it means for "us"? I can tell you that right now. But for you, the man who was supposed to be able to read my very soul like no-one else, it must be obvious, isn't it? Come on, Leo, don't be naive. There's no "four-letter miracle". There is only a six-letter logical conclusion, and we've trembled in the face of it so many times before. We've put it off, suppressed it, written straight past it. But now it has caught up with us, and it's down to me to spell it out: T-H-E E-N-D.

CHAPTER NINE

Three months later

Subject: Yes, it's me

Hello Leo. The well-qualified lady who looks after my
ragged psyche thinks I can afford to ask you how you are.
So, how are you? What can I tell my attentive therapist? I
can't tell her: THIS E-MAIL ADDRESS HAS CHANGED...!

All best
Emmi

Three days later

Subject: Me again

Hi Leo,

I've just been speaking on the phone to my therapist and I
read out the e-mail I sent you on Tuesday. She says I
shouldn't be at all surprised not to have had a response. I
said: "But I'm not surprised." And then she said: "But you
want to know how he is, don't you?" Me: "Yes." Her: "Then
you have to ask him in a way that might give you a chance
of finding out." Me: "Oh, I see. So what's the best way of

doing that?" Her: "Try being friendly." Me: "But I don't feel like being friendly." Her: "Yes you do, you're feeling more like being friendly than you want to admit to yourself. You just don't want him to think that you're feeling like being friendly towards him." Me: "I don't care what he thinks." Her: "You don't really believe that!" Me: "You're right. You're good at seeing straight through people." Her: "Thanks, it's my job." Me: "So what should I do, then?" Her: "First of all, do whatever you think is best for you. Secondly, ask him how he is, but nicely."

Five minutes later

Subject: Me yet again

Hello Leo,

So I'm going to ask you nicely: "How are things?"

I can be even more friendly and say: "Hello Leo, how are you?"

I could even go one step higher on the friendliness scale with: "My *dear* Leo, how are you, how *are* you, how *is* everything with you, how was Christmas, I hope the New Year has got off to a good start, what are you up to these days, how is your love life, how's 'Pam', sorry *Pameeela*?"

Best possible wishes ever,
Emmi

Subject: Me for a third time

Hello Leo,

It's me again. Please forget the nonsense I sent you earlier. But let me tell you something. (That's one of my favourite Leo quotes; I always imagine you blind drunk when you're saying it.) Let me tell you something: Writing does me the world of good!

Tomorrow I'll tell my therapist that I've written to him, and that writing does me good. She'll say to me: "But that was only half the truth." And I'll say: "What was the whole truth, then?" She'll say: "It would have been more accurate to write: Writing to YOU does me the world of good." And I'll say: "But I don't write to anyone else. So if I write that writing does me good, I mean automatically that writing to HIM does me so much good." She'll say: "But he's not to know that." Me: "Yes he will – he knows me." Her: "I'd be very surprised. You don't even know yourself, that's why you've ended up with me." Me: "So what's your hourly rate for insults like this one, then?"

Everything around me is in a state of flux; only the letters that make up these words are the same. It does me good to hold (myself) onto them. It feels as though by doing so, I'm being true at least to myself. I'm not expecting you to reply. In fact I think it's probably best if you don't. The train we were both on has left the station, and "Boston" (and everything leading up to it) threw me off track with a year-long delay. And now I'm sitting in a dingy compartment in a completely new carriage, trying to get my bearings. I have no idea where I'm heading; the stations have no names and even the direction we're going in is rather unclear. When I look out through the small, frosted-glass window at the landscape racing by, I'd like to be able to tell you from time to time whether I see anything familiar, and what that might be. Would that be O.K.? I know you keep a good record of my impressions. And if you'd like to tell me about your own journey sometime – about your experiences aboard the "Pam Express" – I'm all ears. Well, bye then, and make sure you dress warmly. Winter seems to be on the way again. Cold, train air can give you a stiff neck and restrict your range of vision. You can only look straight ahead to your supposed destination, not to either side where those moments happen which make the journey worthwhile.

Emmi

Two days later

Subject: Just tell me ...

... whether you

a.) Delete my e-mails without reading them

b.) Read my e-mails and then delete them

c.) Read them and save them

d.) Don't get any e-mails from me at all

Five hours later

Re:

c

Subject: Good choice!

That was the best choice you could have made, Leo! And how elaborately you've described, justified and formulated it! Erm, has the effort of replying given you carpal tunnel syndrome, or is there something else on the way?

Best wishes
Emmi

Two days later

Subject: Analysis of "c"

Hi Leo,

You must have known the extent to which your first and only offering from the alphabet in sixteen weeks would lend wings to my fantasies. What could Leo the Language Psychologist possibly have wanted to say with an answer like that? What did he expect to achieve by it?

a.) With that most minuscule written sign of life, was he hoping to gain a place in my personal book of Leo records?

b.) Is he captivated by the notion that the recipient of the "c" will spend at least an hour with her therapist pondering the difference between "c" followed by full stop, "c" with a full stop and bracket, and "c" stripped bare, *au naturel*, as Leike created it?

c.) Was "dropping me a line" in this perfectionist, minimalist way an attempt to come across (yet again) as more interesting than the situation warranted?

d.) Or was it purely content-driven? Was he trying to say: Yes, I am reading Emmi's e-mails, I'll even keep saving them, but I'm definitely not going to go on writing to her? And I'm being polite and telling her so. I'm sending her a signal, a feeble signal, but at least it's a signal, even if it's the smallest signal possible, still, it's a signal. I'm sending her a chicken's toe ring with a bite taken out of it. Was that it?

In joyful expectation of another "letter" from you,
Emmi

Three hours later

Re:

A question of my own, dear Emmi: When you say THE END so definitively (as you last did sixteen weeks ago, the day after... you might remember what it was the day after), what do you actually mean?

a.) THE END?

b.) THE END?

c.) THE END?

d.) THE END?

And why can't you stick with either a.), b.), c.) or d.)?

Thirty minutes later

Re:

1.) Because I like writing

2.) O.K.: because I like writing to YOU.

3.) Because my therapist says it does me good, and she should know, she studied it.

4.) Because I was curious to know how long you would manage not to write to me.

5.) Because I was even more curious what your answer would be. (I admit, I'd never have guessed it would be "c".)

6.) Because I was and still am even *more* curious to find out how you were.

7.) Because these kinds of curiosities for external things improve the air around here, the atmosphere in my tiny, sterile, empty new flat with the silent piano and bare walls, which keep on flinging baffled question marks in my face. A flat which has set me back fifteen years in one fell swoop, but without making me fifteen years younger as a result. And now, at thirty-five, I'm at the bottom of a twenty-year-old's stairwell. Which means I've got to climb all those stairs again.

8.) Where were we? Oh yes, at "The End", and why I don't mean "The End" when I say it: because there are certain things I see quite differently from how I saw them sixteen weeks ago, if perhaps less conclusively.

9.) Because the end doesn't quite mean the end doesn't quite mean the end doesn't quite mean the end, Leo. Because in the end each end is also a beginning.

Have a nice evening. And thanks for writing!
Emmi

Ten minutes later

Re:

What? Have you moved out, Emmi? Have you and Bernhard separated?

Two hours later

Re:

I've moved out, I've stepped back a little. I've put some distance between myself and Bernhard. The physical space that separates us now reflects the kind of relationship he and I have had for the past two years. I'm trying to ensure that the children don't suffer as a result. I still want to be there for them whenever they need me. The new circumstances are awful for Jonas. You should see his face when he asks me why I never spend the night at home any more. I say: "Papa and I aren't getting along very well at the moment." Jonas says: "But at night that shouldn't make any difference." And I say: "It does when all that separates you is a thin wall." He says: "Then I'll swap bedrooms with you. I don't mind if there's only a thin wall between me and Papa." What is one supposed to say to that?

Bernhard recognizes his failings and deficiencies. He's ashamed. He's contrite, defeated, completely wiped out. He's trying to salvage what he can, while I try to identify if there is anything that can be salvaged. We've talked so much over the past few months, but unfortunately it's come several years too late. We've peeped behind the facade of our relationship for the very first time, and it looks musty and desolate. It's never been worked on, never cleaned, never aired, everything in a state of decay. Can we ever make amends?

We also talked a lot about you, Leo. But I'll only tell you what we said if you really want to know. (The fact that you'll obviously want to know means that we'll stay in e-mail contact. That's my cunning plan!) I don't want to put any pressure on you, but my therapist is convinced that you're very good for me. She says: "I really don't understand why you spend so much money on sessions with me. You get it all for nothing with your Leo Leike. So why don't you do yourself a favour and make more of an effort with him!" So I'm doing myself a favour and making more of an effort with you, Leo dear. And you're extremely welcome to make a bit more of an effort with me in return.

Goodnight.

The following evening

Subject: (no subject)

Dear Emmi

I'm flattered your psychotherapist thinks I'm capable of replacing her. ("For nothing" would be too cheap, of course, but I'd make you an excellent offer.) And naturally I'm delighted that she, at least, is convinced I'm good for you. But would you be so kind as to ask her whether she can give me assurances that you're good for me too?

Lots of love,
Leo.

One hour later

Re:

She's only thinking about my wellbeing, Leo, not yours. If you don't know what's good for you and want to find out, you'll have to get your own therapist. I highly recommend it, by the way, but you'd probably think it too extravagant.

Have a nice evening,
Emmi

P.S.: Oh, by the way Leo, I'd love to hear how you are. Can't you tell me anything? Won't you drop a few hints, at least?

Please!!

Half an hour later

Re:

Hint 1: I've had a cold for three weeks.

Hint 2: I've only got three more weeks on my own.

Hint 3: Pamela ("Pam") is coming. And staying.

Ten minutes later

Re:

Well, that's a surprise! Congratulations, Leo, and richly deserved! (I'm referring to "Pam", of course, not the cold.)

Best regards,
Emmi

Five minutes later

Re:

I'm reminded of the question we asked each other some months back, but never answered. It was: Did anything change as a result of our meeting? For my part, yes! Ever since I've been able to picture your face when reading your messages, I can guess much more quickly the mood you're in when you write to me, and what your words actually mean when they quite definitely mean something different from what they say on the screen. I can see your lips as they release the words. I can picture your eyes avoiding mine, giving a commentary to what's happening. Just now you wrote, "Well, that's a surprise! Congratulations, Leo, and richly deserved!" What you actually meant was, "Well, that's a disappointment! But it's your own fault, Leo, you obviously don't deserve anything better." Jokingly, you added in brackets, "I'm referring to 'Pam', of course, not the cold." A bitter and twisted comment which I read as, "Better to have a cold for three weeks than that 'Pam' for the rest of your life!" Am I right?

Three minutes later

Re:

No, Leo – I may at times be bitter, but I'm not twisted. I'm sure "Pam" is an amazing woman, and I'm sure she's a good thing for you, better than hay fever any day. Could you send me a photograph of her?

One minute later

Re:

No, Emmi.

Thirty seconds later

Re:

Why not?

Two minutes later

Re:

Because I don't know what you could possibly want with it.
Because it should make no difference to you what she looks
like. Because I don't want you comparing your appearance
to hers. Because I'm tired. Because I'm going to bed now.

Goodnight Emmi.

One minute later

Re:

You sound sulky and irritable, Leo. Why? 1.) Am I getting
on your nerves? 2.) Aren't you happy? 3.) Or don't you have
a photograph of her?

Twenty seconds later

Re:

No.

Yes I am.

Yes I do.

Goodnight!

CHAPTER TEN

The following evening

Subject: Apology

Sorry if I was surly. I'm not going through my best phase at the moment. I'll be in touch.

Love,
Leo

Two hours later

Re:

No problem. Get in touch again whenever you feel like it. You don't have to be at your best. I'd be quite happy with second best.

Emmi

Subject: My mood

Dear Emmi

Why is it that for the last three days I've had this (sometimes really agonizing) feeling that you're waiting impatiently for me to explain just why I'm not at my best at the moment?

Four hours later

Re:

Probably because you're desperate to explain it. If you *are* desperate, just get on with it, stop beating about the bush.

Ten minutes later

Re:

No, Emmi. I'm not at all desperate to explain it! I can't explain it to you, you see, because I can't even explain it to myself. Paradoxically, however, I feel as if I owe you an explanation. Can you explain that?

Eight minutes later

Re:

No idea, Leo. Perhaps you've become paranoid, perhaps you feel you *have* to explain whatever phase you're going through. (A new trait, by the way.) If you like, I can ask my therapist if she's come across any decent phase-explanation-paranoia specialists.

A suggestion to help you relax: I'm not asking you to explain why you aren't "at your best at the moment". I already know.

Three minutes later

Re:

Terrific, Emmi. Go on, explain it to me then, please!

Twenty minutes later

Re:

You're agitated about "...", O.K., about Pamela. You were her guest in Boston. She was your guest after Boston. Or you switched between roles of host and guest in London or wherever else you happened to be. But now the geographical and romantic parameters of the relationship have changed. She's coming to live with you. A long-distance relationship will become a close relationship. Meaning everyday life for two people in their own four walls rather than full board at some boutique hotel. Cleaning windows and rehanging washed curtains rather than gazing out wistfully upon an expanse of fairy-tale landscape. By the way, she's not just coming to you. She's coming *because* of you. She's coming *for* you. She's counting on you. You're taking all the responsibility. And the thought of that is stressing you out. You fear the uncertainty, the deflating feeling that all of a sudden everything could be different between you. Your anxiety is perfectly understandable, and justifiably so, Leo. You can't possibly be "at your best" at the moment. How could you then describe the phase of life you're now approaching, what would that say about your future?

You'll work it out between you somehow, I'm sure of it!

Lots of love, and have a nice evening
Emmi

Seven hours later

Subject: Dearest diary

Hello Emmi,

You'll be asleep by now. I'm guessing it's two or three in the morning. I've been off the drink for a while, so I can't take it. This is only my third glass and everything looks blurry. O.K., I admit it's a large glass. The wine is 13.5 per cent, it says so on the label, it's in my head already, the remaining 86 or 87 per cent is still in the bottle. I'm going to drink it now, there's no alcohol left in it. It's all in my head. But it is the second bottle, if I'm going to be honest.

Emmi, I've got something I need to tell you, you're the only woman I write to, you're the only woman I write to, who I write to about how I write, how I am, how I feel. In fact you're my diary, but you don't keep still like a diary. You're not as patient. You're always interfering, you retaliate, you contradict me, you confuse me. You're a diary with a face, body and shape. You think I can't see you, you think I can't feel you. Wrong. Wrong. How wrong. When I write to you I bring you very close to me. It's always been like that. And ever since I've known you "personally", you know, since we sat opposite each other, since then – thank God nobody has taken my pulse – since then . . . I've never told you, I never wanted to, what's the point? You're married, he loves you.

He made a big mistake, he kept quiet. The biggest mistake, in fact. But you have to forgive him. You belong to your family, and I'm not saying that because I've got conservative values, because I haven't got conservative values... well, maybe my values are a bit conservative, but I'm not conservative, not at all. Where were we? That's right, Emmi, you belong to your family, because that's precisely where you belong, in your family. And I belong to Pamela, or she to me, doesn't matter. No, no, I'm not going to send you a photograph of her. I won't do it, I'd find it too... I'd be subjecting her to too much scrutiny, do you understand me, Emmi, why would I do that? She's different from you, Emmi. But she loves me and we've made a decision, we'll be happy, we suit each other well, we have a future, take my word for it. Can I write that to you? Are you cross with me?

You and me, Emmi, we ought to have stopped all this long ago. This is no way to keep a diary, it's intolerable. You're always looking at me — you would write you're always looking at me so, so, so... And I can see you looking at me when you say so, so, so. It doesn't matter what I say, it doesn't matter if I shut up for as long as I like, you're still looking at me with your eyes/words. Every letter of your every word winks at me so, so, so, like so, like so, like so. Every syllable carries your gaze.

Emmi, Emmi, what a bad winter that was. No Merry Christmas or Happy New Year from Emmi Rothner. I really thought it was over. After that night, you wrote THE END. That night, and then THE END – not the end, but THE END – well, that was too much. I wrote you off. Everything vanished, nothing was left. No diary. No day. It was a horribly empty time, let me tell you. But Pamela loves me, of that I am sure.

Emmi, let me ask you, do you remember that night? We ought not to have done it. You were so angry, so bitter, so sad and yet so, so, so . . . Your breath on my face, in my eyes, it got under my skin. Could intimacy ever get more intimate? How often I had dreamed of that, always the same images. To be in such a close embrace and then to be turned to stone forever . . . And to feel nothing but your breath.

But I'd better stop writing now. I'm slightly drunk, the wine is strong, with or without the alcohol. Fifteen nights to go, Emmi, I've counted them, then Pamela's here. Then my new life will start, you say "phase", I say life. But I don't have conservative values, or just a bit. Your life is Bernhard and the children. Don't cut yourself off. People who live their lives in phases lose the span, the scope, the meaning of the whole. They live in limp, meaningless little bits. In the end they miss out on everything. Cheers!

And now, what the heck, now I'm going to give you a kiss, my dear diary. Don't look at me like that!!! And please excuse e-mails like this. I'm not at my best at the moment, not even second best. And I'm slightly drunk. Not very, but slightly. So. Full stop. Finish. Send. The end, not THE END, just the end.

Yours,
Leo

The following morning

Subject: Fourteen nights to go

Dear Leo

Your drunken outpourings are quite something! That was more than a flood of words, it was a proper torrent. You always let so much swirl about together. And yet sometimes when your closets burst open and your words are soaked in red wine, you can be quite the philosopher. Your observations about conservatism and life phases – the old teachers could learn something from those. I don't know how to begin to respond. I don't even know whether I *should* begin to respond. Is it worth it, for fourteen nights? I'll have to ask my therapist. And you, you can get all that alcohol out of your head!

Lots of love
Your ever-interfering diary

Nine hours later

Re: Our schedule

Good evening Leo,

Have the words on the screen stopped swimming? (Can you see my face in them?) If so, I have the following question, in my capacity as diary, concerning our schedule for the next two weeks (which could well be our last): What shall we do?

1.) Shall we do nothing, so that you can prepare for the arrival of "Pam" in peace? (And I quote: "But she loves me and we've made a decision, we'll be happy, we suit each other well." Incidental comment from Emmi: what a great decision!)

2.) Shall we keep writing to each other, as if there's never been anything between you and your diary (and for that reason alone there never could be)? And our correspondence will cease the moment the plane lands from Boston, so that you can concentrate on the rest of your life, while I plunge into the next phase of mine or repeat the preceding one because my performance in it was mediocre?

3.) Or shall we meet one more time? You know, one of our notorious final meetings. Because, because, because . . . because nothing. Just because. What did we call it last summer? – "A fitting conclusion." Shall we conclude this once and for all? I don't think there'll ever be a better opportunity.

The following evening

Subject: Thirteen nights to go

Hi Leo,

I see that you have opted for 1.) without even consulting your diary. Or are you still thinking about it? Or are you just sober and silent? Come on, tell me!

Emmi

Two hours later

Re:

Sober, silent and entirely at a loss.

Ten minutes later

Re:

If you're sober, drink. If you're silent, say something.
If you're at a loss, ask me. That's what your diary is for.

Re: What should I be asking you?

Re:

Preferably ask me whatever it is that you want to know. And if you're at a loss to the extent that you don't know what you should ask because you haven't a clue what you want to know, then ask me something else. (I learned how to construct sentences like that from you!)

Re:

O.K., Emmi. What are you wearing?

Re:

Well done, Leo! Considering you haven't a clue what you want to know, that was a good, perfectly valid, and – one might even say – burning question!

Re:

Thank you. (I learnt these questions from you!) So what are you wearing right now?

Five minutes later

Re:

What are you expecting me to say? Nothing? Or rather: "Nothing!"? I hope you can live with the sad truth: I'm wearing a grey flannel pyjama top. I've lost the bottoms that go with it, so I've replaced them with a light-blue pair which keep falling down because the elastic's gone. But I feel sorry for them because they're on their own now. One foggy November night, the top that matches them went on ahead, in the washing machine at 90 degrees. To spare myself the sight of my pyjama combo, I'm also wearing a coffee-bean-brown towelling dressing-gown from Eduscho. Does that make you feel better in yourself?

Fifteen minutes later

Re: And if we do meet again, Emmi, what do you imagine might happen?

Three minutes later

Re:

There you go, you see? This last question shows a marked improvement on the previous one. You must have been inspired by my outfit.

Two minutes later

Re:

Go on, what do you imagine might happen?

Eight minutes later

Re:

You can say "will", Leo, you don't have to keep forcing yourself to say "might". I realize you're far from wanting to meet me a fourth time. And I do understand that completely. With "Pam" just around the corner, I expect you're terrified of another night-time sex attack from me, which you might not want to have to fend off. (You're not the only one who likes the conditional tense!) But I can put your mind at rest: that's not what I imagine "might" happen this time, dear Leo.

One minute later

Re:

So what then?

Fifty seconds later

Re:

The way you imagine it.

Thirty seconds later

Re:

But I'm not imagining anything, Emmi, at least not anything in particular.

Twenty seconds later

Re:

That's just what I'm imagining too.

Fifty seconds later

Re:

I don't know, dear Emmi. If I'm being honest, I somehow can't imagine that a "final" meeting would be a good idea if neither of us can imagine what might happen. I think we ought to stick to writing. That way we can allow ourselves to be more expansive with our imagination.

Forty seconds later

Re:

There you go again, dear Leo. Now you're not coming across as the least bit clueless. Or silent. But still sober, unfortunately. I don't think I'll ever get used to that. Goodnight, sleep well. I'm shutting down now.

Thirty seconds later

Re:

Goodnight, Emmi.

The following evening

Subject: Twelve nights to go

Hi Leo,

My therapist has explicitly and emphatically advised me not to meet you in this current phase (which is neither your best nor my second best). Have you two been talking?

Two hours later

Subject: Am I right?

You're there. Am I right?

And you read my e-mail. Am I right?

You just don't know what to say any more. Am I right?

Because you don't have a clue what to do with me. Am I right?

You're thinking to yourself: Dear God, I wish these twelve nights were over! Am I right?

Forty minutes later

Re:

Dear Emmi

Hard though it is for me to admit, I'm afraid every word you say is correct.

Three minutes later

Re:

That's so grim!

One minute later

Re:

Not just for you!

Fifty seconds later

Re:

Shall we stop, then?

Thirty seconds later

Re:

Yes, it would be for the best.

Thirty seconds later

Re:

What, right now?

Forty seconds later

As far as I'm concerned, yes, right now!

Twenty seconds later

Re:

O.K.

Fifteen seconds later
Re:
O.K.

Thirty seconds later
Re:
You first, Leo!

Twenty seconds later
Re:
No, Emmi, you first!

Fifteen seconds later
Re:
Why me?

Twenty-five seconds later
Re:
It was your idea!

Three minutes later
Re:
But you've inspired me, Leo! You've been an inspiration for some days! You and your silence. You and your sobriety. You and your cluelessness. You and your: "It would be for the

best." You and your: "It would be better if we stopped . . ."
You and your: "I think we should leave it now." You and
your: "Dear God, I wish these twelve nights were over!"

Four minutes later

Re:

You put that last sentence in my mouth, my dear.

One minute later

Re:

If I didn't put sentences into your mouth, nothing would
come out at all, dear Leo!

Three minutes later

Re:

The melodramatic way in which you're conducting this
farewell countdown makes me nervous, dear Emmi. Subject:
Fourteen nights to go. Subject: Thirteen nights to go.
Subject: Twelve nights to go. What painful subject-
fetishism, what extreme masochism! Why are you doing it?
Why are you making it more difficult than it already is by
the fact that it is what it is?

Three minutes later

Re:

If I didn't make it more difficult, it wouldn't be any easier.
Please let me go on counting down our last nights together

(sort of), Leo dear. It's my way of coping. And anyway, there aren't that many of them left. And tomorrow morning there'll be one fewer. In other words: your persistently provocative diary bids you a good twelfth-last night.

CHAPTER ELEVEN

The following day

Subject: A suggestion!

Good morning, dear Emmi. Let me make a suggestion for our virtual schedule for the next ten days: Each of us may ask the other one question per day and must answer the other's question. Agreed?

Twenty minutes later

Re:

How did you hit upon that ludicrous idea, my love?

Three minutes later

Re:

Was that your question for today, dearest?

Five minutes later

Re:

Hang on, Leo, I never said I would agree to it. You know I like games — otherwise I wouldn't have been sitting here for the past two years. But this game is totally half-baked. What would we do if, for example, your answer to my question prompted a follow-on question?

One minute later

Re:

You could ask that the following day.

Fifty seconds later

Re:

That's not fair! All you want is for the period between myself and "Pam" to pass more quickly, so that you can be rid of the correspondence between you and your diary at last.

Forty seconds later

Re:

Sorry, Emmi, that's the way the game works. I know because I invented it. Shall we start?

One minute later

Re:

Just a sec. Am I allowed *not* to answer questions?

Fifty seconds later

Re:

No, there's to be no not answering of questions! Answers can be evasive, at a pinch.

Thirty seconds later

Re:

In that case you've got an unfair advantage: you've been in training for the past twenty-five months.

Forty seconds later

Re:

Shall we start now, Emmi love?

Thirty seconds later

Re:

What if I say no?

Two minutes later

Re:

Well, that would be your question and your answer for today. And we'd read each other again tomorrow.

Re:

If you weren't the same Leo Leike I had seen with my very own eyes (but also with entirely different eyes) languishing at a café table, trying his best to be so charming that he could rival even my fantasy of him, then I might say: You're a sadist! Go on, then, ask me a question. (But please, not one about what I'm wearing!)

Emmi

Three hours later

Subject: Question number one

I'm still waiting for your first question, my love. Can't you think of anything? That wasn't my question, by the way! My question is: "Dear Leo, in one of your most recent booze-sodden declarations about you and P...P...Pamela, you said that the two of you were well suited. How? I would be grateful for an explanation."

Five minutes later

Re:

My question to you, Emmi, is: "Would you do it again?"

Fifteen minutes later

Re:

Very clever, Leo. So, I can choose my "it", and God forbid that I should choose the wrong one, because I'd be stuck with "it" forever, even though you're the one enquiring about "it". If you were not Leo but just some other man, it would be quite obvious that "it" could only refer to sex. In our case, my "visit" to your flat, my disappointment, my desperation, my destructiveness, and the "it" that was a consequence of it. If you meant *that* "it", then my answer would have to be no. No, I wouldn't do it again. I wish I hadn't done it in the first place.

But since you *are* Leo Leike, your "it" couldn't have been referring to sex, but to something else, something bigger, something sublime, something of much higher value. If I'm not completely mistaken, your "it" must refer to our correspondence. You ask: "Would you do it again? Would you write back to me again? Would you get involved with me in the same way a second time, with the same intensity and emotional effort? Would you do "it" even if you knew how "it" would turn out?

Yes, Leo. More please. YES! Again and again.

And now it's your turn!

Fifty minutes later

Re:

I know you don't feel like answering my question, but you have to, Leo. You're the one who invented this game!

One hour later

Re:

My answer, dear Emmi, is: "Pamela and I are well suited because I feel that we chime well together. The way we relate to each other is easy and uncomplicated. If both of us do exactly what we want, neither of us is doing anything that the other doesn't want to do. We have similar personalities, both of us are fairly quiet and measured, we don't wind each other up, don't demand more from each other than we are prepared to give ourselves, don't want to change each other, we take each other as we are. We never tire of each other. We like the same music, the same books, films, food and art, have the same attitude to life, the same sense of humour, or lack of it. In short, we get on, and want to be together." That's what I meant by being "well suited".

Goodnight, Emmi.

The following evening

Subject: ???

Hello Emmi, my question for today is: "Why are you not e-mailing me?"

Ten minutes later

Re:

Hi Leo,

My (easy and uncomplicated) answer for today is: "If you re-read the e-mail you wrote yesterday evening about being well suited, you'll understand why I'm not writing to you."

Fifteen minutes later

Subject: Today's question

O.K., let's get this over with. My question is: "Am I right in thinking that you don't actually *want* me to like 'Pam', and that you're not giving me the chance to be well disposed towards your partnership. If you were, you wouldn't be presenting me with a picture of the two of you that leaves me no other option but to creep into my monitor and yell from the depths of my heart: Yeeeeuuch, how revolting! They like the same music, the same books, films, food and art, they have the same views, the same sense of humour, or rather, even worse, the same lack of a sense of humour. Eeeek! Maybe in a few weeks' time they'll be heading off to the golf course in matching blue-and-white-striped socks for a synchronized tee-off. But hey, the two of them will never *ever* ever get bored of each other. Incredible! How on earth do they do it? Listening to Leo describing his compatibility with "Pam" is enough to send me straight to sleep. (Did you get my question? It was somewhere near the beginning.)

Twenty minutes later

Re:

You can be as cynical and mocking as much as you like, Emmi. I never claimed to be exciting. If my descriptions send you to sleep, then at least you're calming down a little; it can only be good for your blood pressure. A minor observation, Emmi – your therapist can corroborate this – it is incredibly unhelpful and even a bit cheap to let a man's train pull out of the station (your words) and then have a go at the woman who's sitting with him in a new carriage. You'll never be able to put me off her like that. On the contrary, you're giving her good publicity.

Which brings me to my answer to your question, which was almost drowned by your emotional monsoon. I have no influence over whether you're "well disposed" towards my

134

"partnership", Emmi. I'd rather you were. But if it makes you feel better not to be, then don't be. I can cope with that. If something should make my partnership with Pamela suffer or fail, it would definitely not be your being ill-disposed towards it.

Enjoy your evening,
Leo

Ten minutes later

Re:

That was unkind, Leo! When I'm being cynical, then at least that's all I am. When you're cynical you can be really nasty.

And by the way, it wasn't ME who let your train pull out of the station, my love. At the time I wrote "the train we were both on has left the station". There's a difference. You're making out that I single-handedly dispatched your train, sending you off to damnation. (And by that I don't mean "Pam"!) The fact is, you and I both allowed our train to speed away. It was a highly polished team effort, after months and months of practising hard at how to miss our station. Please don't forget that.

Goodnight.

Three minutes later

Re:

I take back the matching stripy socks. That was mean.

One minute later

Re:

But you enjoyed it.

Twenty seconds later

Re:

You're right, I really did!

Thirty seconds later

Re:

It fulfilled its purpose then. Sleep well, my dear mockery-maker!

Twenty seconds later

Re:

You too, my beloved mockery-swallower! That's what I really like about you: you appreciate a joke, even when it's at your expense.

Forty seconds later

Re:

Because I like to see you laugh. And nothing seems to delight you more than a joke at my expense.

Thirty seconds later

Re:

Hey Leo, I love stripy socks, by the way! I'm sure you'd look cute in them. Even more innocent than usual.

Goodnight!

The following day

Subject: My question

Dear Emmi,

My question for today is: "Where do you and Bernhard go from here?"

Five minutes later

Re:

No, Leo! Do I have to?

Seven hours later

Subject: Bernhard

O.K., then. At Easter he's flying with me to La Gomera in the Canaries for a week, without the children. I stress: *he* is flying with *me*, I am not flying with him. Although we'll be on the same plane. I'm going to let it happen. I think it's courageous of him. He can't expect anything, and yet he expects everything. He believes he can reconquer my feelings, that our great love will be reawakened, embedded in sand, salt, suncream and stones. Ah well. Maybe I'll get my sailing licence.

Five minutes later

Re:

Does that mean you're giving your marriage another chance?

Three minutes later

Re:

Steady on, my dear Leo! Only one question per day!

Two minutes later

Re:

O.K., I'll ask you again tomorrow. So what's your question?

Four minutes later

Re:

I'm saving it for prime-time. I've already seen the thriller that's on tonight.

Five hours later

Subject: My question

This is my question: "Can you still feel it?"

Two hours later

Re:

You have to answer every question, Leo dear!

Re:

Coward! You could at least admit that you have no idea what "it" is, the thing you're supposed to be able to feel. At least that would be a stylish way of skirting around the fact that you can't feel it at all any more. Because if you did, you'd know what "it" is. But take comfort, I didn't expect you to. It's late, I'm off to bed.

Goodnight. Seven more waking ups and then we're done.

Emmi

Twenty minutes later

Subject: Of course I can!

Hi Emmi,

I've just got in. In answer to your question: "Yes, of course I can still feel it."

Goodnight,
Leo

Three minutes later

Re:

Leo, wait! I'm (suddenly) wide awake again and I'm afraid I'm not going to let you just slink off to bed like that, even at this late hour. I won't allow it; it's against all the rules! "Yes, of course I can still feel it" is a nothing statement. That's no answer, not even an evasive one. You've given me no evidence to suggest that you know what "it" is, the thing you're supposed to be able to feel. You're probably just bluffing, to get a bit of peace and quiet. But I'm sorry, Leo dear, you still owe me a proper answer!

Fifteen minutes later

Re:

My answer was as cryptic as your question, dear Emmi. You didn't call "it" by its name because you wanted to test me, to see whether I remembered what "it" was. I didn't call "it" by its name because I wanted to test you to see whether you'd believe (you didn't!) that I knew what I was talking and thinking about, and what I was feeling when I think of you. "It", for instance. Yes, I still can. Sometimes the feeling's stronger, sometimes weaker. Sometimes I have to expose it first with the tip of my middle finger. Sometimes I stroke it with the thumb on my other hand. For the most part it makes itself known. I can run as much water over it as I like, it won't wash away, it keeps on coming back. Sometimes it tickles, which probably means you're writing me a cynical e-mail. And sometimes it really hurts, which means I'm missing you, Emmi, and wishing that everything were different. But I don't want to be ungrateful. I have "it", the point where you touched me in the centre of my palm. All my memories and desires are crammed into it. This point houses the full Emmi catalogue, with every conceivable accessory for the demanding, gazing-out-wistfully-upon-an-expanse-of-fairy-tale-landscape Leo Leike.

Goodnight!

Re:

Thanks Leo, I enjoyed that! I'd love to be with you right now!

One minute later

Re:

You are!

The following day

Subject: My question

Hello Emmi. As promised, I'm going to repeat my question from yesterday: "Are you giving your marriage another chance?"

Two hours later

Re:

How very exciting! After romantic, night-time Leo, who can be so, so, so engaging when he talks about points of contact, here we have sober day-time Leo again, the e-mail pastor who fights on behalf of the relationships of his confidantes as if he could earn a commission from them. Hmmm. I'm going to interpose a question. Here goes: "In some of the very first messages after the resumption of my Leo-mail relationship I wrote that I had talked to Bernhard about you a great deal, about both of us, in fact. Why aren't you asking me what was said? Why will you only see Bernhard in isolation? Why can you not grasp that my relationship with him is directly connected to my relationship with you?" (And please don't now tell me that was three questions. There were three question marks, but it's one and the same question!)

Three hours later

Re:

Dear Emmi,

I don't want you to discuss me with Bernhard, or at least, I don't want to know if you do. I'm neither a part of your family, nor of your group of friends. I categorically refuse to believe that your relationship with him has anything to do with your relationship with me. I just don't believe it! I never wanted to fight him. I never wanted to push him out. I never wanted to squeeze myself into your marriage. I didn't want to take a single piece of you away from your husband. And, conversely, I can't bear the idea that for you I was and am no more than a supplement to him. Right from the start, it was only ever either "either" or "or" for me. Meaning that when you said you were "happily married", all that was left for me was "or".

Have a nice evening,
Leo

Twenty minutes later

Re:

A reply, for a change:

1.) Are you telling me that these past two years you've been an "or"? I have to say your "or" is definitely capable of swinging over to the "either" side. And if you can be so "either" when you're an "or", how "either" would you be if you really *were* an "either"?

2.) You write: "I didn't want to take a single piece of you away from your husband." Can't you see that this is exactly the sort of arch-conservative statement I resent. It's utterly degrading. I am not some sort of commodity, the possession of one man that cannot be passed over to another. I OWN MYSELF, Leo, nobody else does. You can't "take me away" from anyone, and no husband in the entire world would ever be able to "keep" me. I'M the only person who can "keep" me or "take me away" from anyone else. Sometimes I give myself away, sometimes I give myself up. But only rarely. And not to just anyone.

3.) You're still fixed on the term "happily married". Have the developments in my life over the past year completely passed you by? Have I not talked about it enough? Do I not refer to it all the time?

4.) Which brings me neatly to your sententious question, laden as it is with strict Catholic optimism: "Are you giving your marriage another chance?" Am I giving our marriage another chance? – I could give you a good answer to that, my love! But I'm going to keep it to myself for the moment. All I want to say for today is: For God's sake, Leo, I really don't care about marriage as an institution! It's just a construct for those who've bought into it to cling to if they feel they're losing their footing. It's the individuals who count. Bernhard is important to me. Bernhard and the children. I feel I have a duty there, I still do. Whether or not this harbours "future prospects" remains to be seen.

5.) I'm hoping for a more exciting question from you tomorrow!!! We only have six nights to go, my love.

6.) Enjoy your evening. I'm off to the cinema.

The following evening

Subject: O.K., exciting

Hello Emmi,

My question is: "How was the cinema, what did you see?" Only joking! My real question: "Do you sometimes think about having sex with me?"

Ten minutes later

Re:

Thank you for that, Leo! You asked that one for my sake, didn't you? You know how much I go for those questions. You only seem to be exercised by such matters when you're in the company of your bottle-shaped mates from Bordeaux. But I have to say, Leo, I'm thrilled that you're behaving as if sex wasn't a taboo subject, even when we're sober. And for that you've earned yourself an honest response: "No, I don't *sometimes* think about sex with you!" I'd love to ask you the same question back, but oddly enough the thought of your soon-to-be-arriving synchronized girlfriend "Pam" has just got in the way. So as far as sex is concerned, I think I'll leave it there with my conservative correspondent, Leo "Either-Or" Leike.

Kiss kiss
Emmi

Thirty seconds later

Subject: Pamela

Very strange. All it takes is for you to write the word "sex",
probably wearing your stripy socks, and I need to down two
glasses of whisky. Sadly my question for you today isn't
nearly as tantalizing. Here it is: "What does Pamela know
about us?" (Note: I've written "Pamela". So I'm expecting an
equally serious answer.)

One minute later

Re:

Nothing!

Two minutes later

Re:

What, nothing at all? Are you being serious?

Ten minutes later

Subject: (no subject)

Dear Leo

I hope you agree that "Nothing!" can't be everything, I
mean, that can't be your whole answer. My question was an
attempt to establish WHY it is that "Pam" knows what she
knows about us, and if it's the case that she knows nothing,
WHY in the world does she not? Well, that's obvious:
because you haven't told her anything. But WHY NOT?
That's my question for today. (No, not tomorrow's, today's!)
And I'm telling you now: if you don't volunteer the answer,

I'll fly up to flat 15 and extract it from you personally. I need it, I need to know, and I need to go and share it with my therapist first thing tomorrow.

One minute later

Re:

I have you here before me, Emmi! Whenever you demand something (from me) with such urgency, you look me straight in the eye and your pupils are transformed into greenish-yellow arrows. You could stab somebody to death with a look like that.

Forty seconds later

Re:

That's a good observation! And before I leap at you with bared teeth, I'll blink three times. One. Two. Two and a quarter. Two and a half ... I'm waiting, Leo!

Ten minutes later

Re:

I didn't tell Pamela anything about us in Boston because I considered our "us" to be a closed matter. And after Boston I didn't tell her anything about us because I hadn't told her anything about us in Boston. I couldn't start in the middle. Either you tell crazy stories like ours from the beginning or not at all.

One minute later

Re:

You could have brought her up to speed.

Forty seconds later

Re:

True.

Fifty seconds later

Re:

But it wouldn't have been worth it, because you wanted to bring this whole "crazy" business with me to an end (or rather, not begin it all over again) as quickly as possible.

Thirty seconds later

Re:

No.

Twenty seconds later

Re:

What do you mean, "No"?

Thirty seconds later

Re:

Your conclusion is wrong.

Forty seconds later

Re:

Then please give me a correct one!

Two minutes later

Subject: (no subject)

No, Leo, not tomorrow! (Watch out, I'm about to leap!)

Three minutes later

Re:

I didn't tell her anything about us because she wouldn't have understood. And if she had understood, then it wouldn't have been the truth. It's impossible to understand the truth about us, you see. I basically don't understand it myself.

Thirty seconds later

Re:

Come on, Leo, of course you understand it. In fact you understand it extremely well. You understand it well enough to keep it to yourself. You don't want to make "Pam" feel insecure.

Forty seconds later

Re:

Perhaps.

One minute later

Re:

But it wouldn't be a good idea to begin a relationship with a woman carrying a secret about a crazy story with someone else, Leo, my love.

Fifty seconds later

The secret is safely hidden away, Emmi dear.

Two minutes later

Re:

Of course, your closets full of feelings. Stuff Emmi in to one of them. Shut the door. Turn the key as far as it goes. Set the temperature inside to minus twenty. Done. And make sure you defrost it every few months. Goodnight. It's cold, I'm getting under the covers.

CHAPTER TWELVE

The following evening

Subject: My question

Dear Emmi,

Are we not going to ask each other a question today? Is the game over? Are you pissed off? (Three question marks, one question – rules as interpreted by Emmi Rothner.)

Two hours later

Subject: My question

What is the truth about us, Leo?

Fifteen minutes later

Re:

The truth about us? You've got a family that you're very fond of, a husband who loves you, and a marriage that's still salvageable. And I've got a relationship that I can build on. Each of us has – a future. It's just that we don't have one together. Viewed realistically, dear Emmi, that's the truth about us.

Three minutes later

Re:

I detest you when you're being realistic!

And by the way, what you've just said is not the truth ABOUT us, it's the truth WITHOUT us. And believe it or not, Leo, I knew it already! It's been embedded in every fifth e-mail I've had from you over the past two years. Right, I'm off out. I'm going for dinner with Philip. Philip? He's a web designer, young, single, makes me laugh. He adores me and I'm in the mood, not for him especially, but for his adoration. That's the truth about Philip and me. If your question for tomorrow were to be "How was your evening with Philip?" I can answer that today, right now in fact: it was very laid-back.

I hope you enjoy *your* evening.

Emmi

Six hours later

Re:

Hello Emmi, it's four o'clock and I can't get to sleep. My question for the day now dawning: "Are we going to see each other one more time?"

That morning

Subject: What for?

Dear Leo,

Isn't it a bit late to be asking a question like that? Barely two weeks ago you were fixed on a radical anti-meeting course, you were totally against it. And I quote: "I somehow can't imagine that a 'final' meeting would be a good idea if neither of us can imagine what might happen." Why now? You're not suddenly imagining that "something" might happen after all, are you? If I've done my sums correctly, Leo, "we" only have three days until "Pam" arrives. Three days to discover a strikingly different truth about us from the one you insist is "realistic". A truth which probably wouldn't go down too well with your girlfriend from Boston, who knows nothing about us, and therefore mustn't find out anything about us. So we have two evenings left for a secret assignation. But why, Leo? What for? Yes, I think that will be my question for today, you could call it my third-last question: WHAT FOR?

Twenty minutes later

Re:

We don't have to meet in the evening, Emmi. I was thinking more of an hour or two one afternoon in a café.

Thirty seconds later

Re:

Oh, I see. Yes. Of course. Leo! Nice. What for?

Forty seconds later

Re:

So I can see you one more time.

Thirty seconds later

Re:

What would you get out of it?

Fifty seconds later

Re:

A good feeling.

Seven minutes later

Re:

I'm delighted for you, but that would be the opposite of how *I'd* feel. Seeing you: fine. Seeing you "one more time", one last time: shit! We've been seeing each other "for the last time" for a year and a half now, Leo! We've been saying goodbye for a year and a half. It seems as though we've got to know each other just so that we can say goodbye. I can't do this any more, Leo. I'm saturated with goodbyes, I'm sick of goodbyes, I'm damaged by goodbyes. Please, just go. Send me your systems manager: at least I can always count on him to e-mail back within ten seconds with his crisp little greeting. But just stop it with your endless goodbyes. And don't now give me that humiliating feeling that you can't think of anything nicer than seeing me "one last time".

Nine minutes later

Re:

I didn't say "one last time", I said "one more time". And even that sounds more dramatic in an e-mail than it is. You wouldn't find it humiliating face to face. In any case, you could never be lost to me. I have so much of you within me. I've always considered that to be an asset. Every sensory impression of Emmi is a bonus. For me, saying goodbye to you means no longer thinking of you, and no longer feeling anything. Believe me, I'm nowhere near saying goodbye.

Five minutes later

Re:

What perfect landing conditions for the woman with whom you're going to spend the rest of your life! Poor Pamela! Thank God she knows nothing of your sensory impressions of Emmi. Just don't show her the keys to your closets of feelings, Leo dear, whatever you do. That would hurt her deeply.

Twelve minutes later

Re:

You can't cheat with feelings alone, Emmi my love. It is only when you act on your feelings and thereby cause someone to suffer that you've done something wrong. And another thing: You really don't have to be sorry for Pamela. My feelings for you don't detract from those I have for her. The two have nothing to do with each other. They aren't in competition. You are quite a different person from her.

I do not have a fixed allocation of feelings that have to be distributed amongst the different people who mean something to me in different ways. Every person who is important to me stands for themselves and occupies their own place within me. I cannot believe it's any different with you.

Fifteen minutes later

Subject: Cheating

Dear Leo,

1.) You don't have to say "person", why not say "woman"? I know who you're talking about.

2.) What do you mean by "acting on your feelings"? You act on your feelings by feeling them. If anything, cheating is hiding in an exchange of feelings the feelings (you feel) for someone else. But take some comfort, Leo, I've only known this since I've been having therapy. I cheated on Bernhard with you, not that particular night, but in the three hundred nights that preceded it. But those times are over. Now he knows everything about you and me. He even knows my "truth about us". It might only be half the truth, but it's my half. And I'm not ashamed of it.

3.) Of course I could congratulate you and show my admiration for the fact that, whatever the size of your heart, there seems to be space enough in it for several closets full of feelings for various different women. But unfortunately I'm thirty-five years old, I've lived through a fair bit and I don't mind saying that this whole business is quite simple. You – yes, even you – like keeping several women in your heart. Better still, you'd like as many (interesting) woman as possible to keep you in their hearts. Of course they're all *soooooo* very different from each other. Each of them is "something quite special". Each stands on her own. And that's no surprise, Leo, because *you're* the one who makes each of them stand alone. When you think of one, you forget all the others. If you open one closetful of feelings, all the others remain firmly locked.

4.) I'm different. My feelings aren't parallel. My feelings are linear. And my love is linear. One after the other. But only ever one at a time. At the moment it's, er, let's say it's Philip. I love the way he smells of Abercrombie & Fitch.

5.) Right, now I'm going to shut down and I'm not booting up again until tomorrow morning. Have a nice third-last afternoon, third-last evening, third-last night, Leo.
I hope you sleep better.

Emmi

Five hours later

Subject: Shocking track record

Dear Emmi,

a.) I'm bored when I'm sober.

b.) I have no sense of humour, even when I've drunk something.

c.) I've been practising evasive answers for two years.

d.) When I feel, I cheat (specifically: you with Pamela, Pamela with you, and both of you with me).

e.) In every fifth e-mail I give you subtle reminders that you and I are both "spoken for", and thus have no future together.

f.) I've been saying goodbye to you for two years.

g.) My powers of attraction are finite. There's absolutely no need for you to see me again.

h.) My life motto is objectionable: "I'd like as many (interesting) women as possible to keep me in their hearts." (Can I make a confession, Emmi? I'll take the uninteresting ones, too. Just so long as there are as many as possible.)

i.) I'm a man.

j.) But I don't smell of that Evercrumby and Fish thingummy.

k.) And so to my penultimate question: WHY ARE YOU STILL WRITING TO ME?

The following morning

Re:

Because I have to answer your penultimate question. Because that's the way the game goes. Because I'm not going to give up so close to the end. Because I never give up. Because I can't lose. Because I don't want to lose. Because I don't want to lose you.

Five minutes later

Subject: And apart from that

And apart from that you write really sweet e-mails. Sometimes.

And it's not often that you're humourless and boring at the same time.

Three minutes later

Subject: What's more

O.K. I never found you boring! (Apart from when you write about what you and "Pam" have in common.) And looks aren't everything, Leo. – That used to be one of your refrains, remember?

Seven minutes later

Subject: O.K., O.K.

Alright, alright, alright, so you *are* good-looking! We know that, everyone knows that! Has that satisfied your vanity?

One hour later

Subject: (no subject)

Fine, Leo, just give it all a little time to sink in.

Subject: My penultimate question

Maybe what you're waiting for is my penultimate question. Here it comes: Are we actually going to stop the day after tomorrow, or will we keep writing to each other? I mean, from time to time, when one of us feels like it? We could still say goodbye to each other to make it official, also for "Pam"'s sake, so that things are clear-cut as far as she's concerned. Oh, but hang on, you're "nowhere near" saying goodbye to me; you're just going to put your feelings on ice for a while. Whatever. Are we going to keep writing? Or would you rather not be disturbed from now on, from "Pam" on, shall we say? Just tell me, and I'll stop looking in my inbox. Or I'll disconnect from the internet. No, that wouldn't work, I've got seven new clients who want me to design their websites – they'd prefer me to do my work online. Whatever. Are we going to keep writing, Leo? Could you do it despite "Pam"? It could be anytime. But are we still going to write?

Re:

Dear Emmi,

Yes, let's. On the condition that you mentioned in your third sentence, "when one of us feels like it". I'm going to be honest with you, Emmi. I can't say whether I'll feel like it, when I'll feel like it, how often I'll feel like it. And if I do feel like it, whether it's a good thing that I actually do it. Never wait for an e-mail from me, please! If one does come, then I felt like it. If it doesn't then maybe I did feel like it, but thought better of it. The converse is also true. We mustn't ever again go mad in expectation of e-mail, or find ourselves feverishly drafting replies. Write to me, Emmi, if you feel like it. And if I feel like it, I'll write back.

Three minutes later

Re:

That e-mail wasn't sweet at all, Leo! But I understand what you're saying. And I'll comply. Enough for today, bye bye. Now I feel like shutting up. Tomorrow is another day. Even if in some respect it will be our last.

The following morning

Subject: Final question

Dear Emmi,

How should I have behaved back then, what should I have done, what would have been better? Back then, when your husband begged me to disappear from your life, not to wreck your marriage, to "save" your family. "Boston" was the only sensible solution, wasn't it? What other decision could I have taken, what would have been the right one? This question has been torturing me for eighteen months. Please tell me!

One hour later

Subject: Final answer

Perhaps you couldn't have made a better decision on your own. But you shouldn't have been making that decision on your own. You should have allowed me to help you make that decision. You should have let me in on the situation with Bernhard, since he was too cowardly to do so himself. It wasn't YOUR responsibility at the time to "save" my marriage, or to end it. It was ours, mine and my husband's! Your secret pact with him, and your mysterious flight to Boston robbed me of the opportunity to take the right steps at the right time. And yes, you should have fought harder for me, Leo. Not like a hero, not like a good guy, not like a "real man", simply like someone who trusts his own feelings. Yes, you're right: we didn't know each other back then, we hadn't even met. So what? I maintain that our relationship was already quite developed. It's true that we hadn't lived together in the traditional sense, but we'd experienced each other, and that counts for more. We were prepared to kiss each other blind, so sure were we of our mutual devotion. So close was our attachment. But you, you wouldn't commit. You gave up on me out of some misplaced sense of chivalry. Without even putting up a fight. THAT'S what you could have done differently. THAT'S what you could have done better, Leo dear!

Ten minutes later

Re:

I wanted the best for you. Unfortunately it never occurred to me that I might be the best. Unfortunately. Pity. Missed opportunity. I'm sorry. I'm really sorry!

Five minutes later

Subject: My last question

Will you come and see me, Leo?

Fifteen minutes later

Subject: (no subject)

Don't be shy to write back.

Five minutes later

Re:

What was that delightful answer you wrote in capital letters
a couple of days ago, when faced with a similar situation?
WHAT FOR?

One minute later

Re:

I don't call that an answer. That's another question, but I'm
afraid you don't have any questions left, my dear. You've
used them all up, on inanities. Now you've got to take a risk.
Will you come over? Or more precisely: will you come over
today? Yes or no.

Twenty minutes later

You're putting up a good show, Leo dear. No "yes". No "no".
And yet this really has to be YOUR decision. You can choose,
you needn't think about it even for a moment.

Three minutes later

Re:

Of course I'm thinking of you. Of you and what you wrote on Thursday. "Seeing you: fine. Seeing you 'one more time', one last time: shit!" That's pretty much the opposite of your position today. Why now, all of a sudden? Why should I come over? If you don't give me an answer, I'll provide one myself.

One minute later

Re:

Your thinking is all wrong, Leo! O.K., when you've made your mind up I'll tell you. So are you coming over to my place, Feldgasse 14, third floor, flat 17? Yes or no?

Eight minutes later

Re:

Yes.

Fifty seconds later

Re:

Really? Are you sure?

Re:

Those were two unauthorized questions. But I'll answer anyway: No, Emmi, I'm not sure. I'm absolutely not sure. I've rarely been this unsure in my life. But I'll risk it.

Two minutes later

Re:

Thank you, Leo! You can put all your various horror scenarios and other visions out of your head. It'll be a short meeting. Ten minutes, let's say. I'd just like to have a whisky with you. Only the one, really! (You could have a glass of red wine instead, if you like.) And then – and that's the real reason for my invitation – I'd like to give you something. The handover won't take longer than five seconds. And then, my dear, you'll be free to go.

One minute later

Re:

What do you want to give me?

Two minutes later

Re:

Something personal. A souvenir. I promise you, there won't be any grief, no scene, no tears. Just a slug of whisky, a little handover. And then: goodbye. It won't hurt. Relative to the situation, I mean. So, come on then!

Forty seconds later

Re:

When?

Thirty seconds later

Re:

At eight?

Forty seconds later

Eight. O.K. Eight o'clock.

Thirty seconds later

Re:

See you at eight, then!

Forty seconds later

See you at eight!

CHAPTER THIRTEEN

Two weeks later

Subject: Signs of life

Hello Emmi, how are you? (It would be nice to be able to use a different phrase for once. But what?) It would do me the world of good to know that you're alright. I think about you often. Whenever . . . I think you know what I mean. Thank you for that!

Leo.

Three days later

Re:

Hi Leo,

Good to hear from you. Did you feel like it, then? Did you really feel like it? Or was it just the usual silence-breaking, separation-pitying, conscience-assuaging, distance-defying crap? Yes, Leo, I'm alright. (Why do you assume, by the way, that the best I can feel is "alright"?). Well, the truth is I don't feel alright enough to ask in return how you are. I don't want to know. Because it wouldn't do me the world

of good if I knew that things were going twice as well for
you than "alright". And I'm assuming that's the case.

Long-distance greetings from,
Emmi

One week later

Subject: Now

Dear Emmi,

Yes, I did rather feel like it.

Night,
Leo.

One day later

Re:

Glad to hear it!

Night,
Emmi

Two weeks later

Subject: What a coincidence!

Hi Leo,

Is "Pam" by any chance a tall, slim, long-legged blonde
beauty? A bit like your sister, Adrienne? About my age?
Two or three years younger, maybe? My accountant's office
is around the corner from your house. (No, Leo, that's not
why I chose him!) And just as I was passing your front
door, one of those lanky, I mean, one of those very tall,

good-looking women with pale make-up shot out of it, like a mail-order model on a shoot for a winter collection. She was so American-looking, the long neck, the tan-coloured shoes, the bulky, square handbag, the chiselled chin and tornado-like jaw movements, the way she chewed gum. I bet that's how people learn how to chew gum in Boston. It must have been "Pam". You can imagine how surprised I was! It's such a small world, don't you think?

BW
Emmi

Three days later

Subject: Pissed off?

Are you pissed off with me, Leo? Don't worry, my next meeting with the accountant isn't for another six months.

One hour later

Dear Emmi,

Obviously I can't demand that you do (or don't do) anything. But I would ask you to refrain from making any more purely coincidental accountant-related reconnaissance trips to my area. What good does it do?

Best wishes,
Leo

P.S. Pamela never chews gum, neither in the North American style, South American style, nor in the style of anywhere else in the world, for that matter.

Three hours later

Re:

It must have been a mouthful of cheeseburger, then. Chill out a little, Leo. You really can't take a joke, can you? So what if I recognize "Pam"? So what if I know her? We might like each other, we might become the best of friends, go on holiday together, compare our diary entries on Leo Leike. And then the three of us could live together in a house-share. Or the five of us, and I could look after the children in the evenings . . . O.K., I'll stop now. I don't think you're finding any of this particularly amusing, are you? Nor am I, to tell the truth, when I get right down to it.

Wishing you pleasant, undisturbed days with plenty of nice terrace time at flat 15.

Your
Emmi

P.S. I'm going on holiday!

One week later

Subject: The seventh wave

Hello Leo,

I'm sitting on my balcony in Playa de Alojera on La Gomera, looking out over the pebbly cove with its black sand and salty tongues of surf, far out to sea and further still, all the way to the horizon separating light blue from dark, sky from water. You can't imagine how beautiful it is here. You two should definitely come some time. It's as if this place was created especially for people who have just fallen in love.

Why am I writing to you? Because I feel like it. And because I don't want to wait for the seventh wave in silence. Yes, here people tell the story of the indomitable seventh wave. The first six are predictable and evenly spaced. Each determines the next, each is created on the back of the other, there are no surprises. They're in rhythm. Six approaches, however different they appear when looked at from afar, six approaches – and always the same destination.

But beware the seventh wave! That's the unpredictable one. For a long time it's inconspicuous, it goes along with the monotonous sequence, blends in with its predecessors. But then sometimes it breaks free. It's only ever that one, the seventh wave. Because it is reckless, artless, rebellious, clearing everything in its path, recreating everything. It has no past, only a now. And afterwards everything is different. Is it better or worse? Only those who have been swept up by this wave, those who have had the courage to face it, to be pulled along in its wake, can make that judgment.

I've been sitting here counting the waves for more than an hour, watching what happens to every seventh one. None of them has broken away yet. But I'm on holiday, I am patient, I can wait. I'm not going to give up hope! Here where I am on the west coast, a warm, strong southerly wind is blowing.

Emmi

Five days later

Subject: Back?

Hello Emmi,

Thanks for your sea-mail. So? Has it done its breaking-the-pattern thing, the seventh wave? Have you let it sweep you up?

Love,
Leo

Three days later

Subject: Every seventh wave

There was something about your story that rang a bell, so I did some research into the seventh wave, Emmi dear. The one-time convict, Henri Charrière, described it in his autobiographical novel *Papillon*. After he was transported to Devil's Island off the coast of French Guiana, he spent weeks observing the sea and noticed that every seventh wave was higher than the others. He used one of those seventh waves – he called it "Lisette" – to drift out to sea on his raft made of bags of coconuts, and thereby made his escape.

But what I wanted to say, in fact, was that I miss you, Emmi.

One day later

Subject: (no subject)

And, in fact, you must have got back some time ago. Are you?

Six days later

Subject: Dead calm

Dear Emmi

I just want to know if everything's alright. You don't have to write back if you don't feel like it. Just write to say that you don't feel like writing to me, if you don't feel like it. And on the off chance that you *do* feel like it, then write! It would make me happy, delighted even! There are no waves here, not the first six. And certainly not the seventh. The sea is calm. It sparkles like a mirror, the sun is dazzling. I'm not waiting for anything. Everything is here, everything is taking its course. No change in sight. Dead calm. Please, Emmi, just a few words from you, at the least.

Leo.

Three days later

Re:

Everything's fine, Leo! I'll write more in a few days. I've been making plans.

Emmi

Eight days later

Subject: A fresh start

Dear Leo,

Bernhard and I are trying to make another go of it. We had a nice, even quite harmonious holiday together. Like they used to be. Well, similar. No, quite different in fact, whatever. We know what we mean to each other. We know what we have together. We know that it's not everything. But now we also know that it doesn't have to be everything. It seems that one person cannot give another everything. Of course you could spend your entire life waiting for someone to come along who could give you everything. You get that wonderful, bewitching, stirring "everything-illusion" that makes your heart pound, that makes it bearable to live with chronic deficiencies, until the illusion is spent. Then all you feel is the deficiency. I've had enough of that feeling. I don't want it any more. I'm no longer striving for an ideal. I just want to make the best of a good thing, that's enough to make me happy.

I'm going to move back home, to Bernhard. He's going to be away quite a lot over the next year or so, he's got some big concert tours coming up. He's very sought after now on an international level. The children are going to need me. (Or do I need the children? Can I still think of them as children? Well, whatever.) I'm going to keep on my little flat as a retreat for my "me" time.

So what of the two of us, Leo? I've thought about it a lot. I've spoken to Bernhard about it too, whether you like it or not. He knows how important you are to me. He knows we've met briefly on a few occasions. He knows that I like you, yes, even on a normal level, physically, unvirtually, with real hands and feet. He knows that I could have imagined everything possible with you. And he knows that I *did* imagine everything possible with you. He also knows that I still rely on your words, and he knows that I have an insatiable need to write to you. Yes, he knows that we're still writing to each other. He just doesn't know WHAT we're writing to each other. And I'm not going to tell him because it has nothing to do with him, only with us and no-one else.

But I'd like to think that even if he did know what we wrote to each other about and the kinds of exchanges we have, he'd find it all perfectly reasonable. I no longer want to deceive him with my unfulfilled longings, my "everything-illusions". I want to end this isolation from you, Leo. I want what you've been wanting all along, if you're honest with yourself: I want – and now I'm dying to know whether I'll be able to get it out – I want, I want, I want . . . us to remain friends. (Did it!) Correspondents. Do you understand? No more pounding hearts. No more tummy aches. No more yearning. No trembling. No hoping. No wishing. No waiting. All I want are e-mails from my friend Leo. And if I don't get them, my world won't come to an end. That's what I want! No more weekly armageddons. Do you understand?

Lots of love
Emmi

Ten minutes later

The seventh wave did get you after all!

Four minutes later

No, Leo, on the contrary. It failed to materialize. I waited for a week. It didn't come. And shall I tell you why? Because it doesn't exist. It was just an "everything-illusion". I don't believe in it. I don't need waves; I don't need the first six, and I definitely don't need the seventh. I'd rather stick with Leo Leike: "The sea is calm. It sparkles like a mirror, the sun is dazzling. I'm not waiting for anything. Everything is here, everything is taking its course. No change in sight. Dead calm." I could live with that. At least it would mean a better night's sleep.

Three minutes later

Re:

I wouldn't set your expectations too high, Emmi. You have to be the right type for calm waters. For some, dead calm is inner peace, for others it's the doldrums.

Two minutes later

Re:

You write as though you're the doldrums type, my friend.

One minute later

Re:

I was actually thinking of you, my friend.

Two minutes later

Re:

That's most considerate of you, Leo. But maybe in the whole scheme of things you should be thinking of yourself instead. Of you and (". . ."). And while we're on the subject, you've been living a whole new life for the past ten weeks, a new life with someone else. But you haven't told me a single

thing about it. Not a peep about your relationship! BUT A
LOYAL PENFRIEND HAS THE RIGHT TO KNOW!

Have a nice evening,
Emmi

Five minutes later

Re:

You ask too much of me, Emmi. You probably don't have a
clue HOW MUCH YOU ASK OF ME! Leo.

Four days later

Re:

Too much, clearly!

Three days later

Re:

Come on, Leo, pull yourself together, make an effort. Tell me
about you and Pamela. Please, please, please! How is she?
How do you find living together? Has she settled in? Does
she feel at home in flat 15? Does she have muesli for
breakfast, or oily tuna sandwiches? Does she sleep on the
right or the left, on her tummy or on her back? How's her
job going? Does she talk about her colleagues? What do you
get up to at the weekend? How do you spend your
evenings? Does she wear tanga briefs or big Boston
bloomers? How often do you have sex? Who initiates it?
Who stops first, and why? What's her handicap? (I'm
referring to her golf.) What else do you get up to? Does she

like *Wiener Schnitzel* and *Apfelstrudel*? What are her hobbies? Pole vaulting? What shoes does she wear? (Other than the tan-coloured ones from Boston.) How long does it take her to blow-dry her blonde hair? What language do you talk to each other in? Does she write you e-mails in English or German? Are you very much in love with her?

The following day

Re:

For breakfast she drinks old Boston white coffee with lots of hot water, milk and sugar, but without the coffee. And she eats bread (no butter) and jam made from Wachau apricots. She sleeps on her right cheek and never dreams about work, thank God. But that's not what you're really interested in. Am I right? So let's get straight to the climax: How often do we have sex? All the time, Emmi, it's non-stop, I'm telling you! We usually start early in the morning (both at the same time) and don't stop, say, for a week. It's really quite hard writing platonic e-mails to Emmi on the side. So your question about her underwear is redundant. And in our rare breaks from sex she blow-dries her knee-length flowing blonde hair.

Have a nice afternoon, dear penfriend!
Leo

Eight minutes later

Re:

That was quite a good answer, Leo. It had a certain pizzazz! See, you can still do it if you try! Have a nice afternoon yourself. I'm off to buy some trousers. With Jonas, unfortunately. For Jonas, in fact! Fashion is so unfair: the people who need the new trousers don't want them (Jonas). The people who want new trousers don't need them (me).

P.S. I still don't know whether you two write e-mails to each other in English or German.

Five hours later

Re:

Neither.

The following day

Re:

Russian?

Ten hours later

Re:

We don't write e-mails. We use the phone.

Three minutes later

Re:

Oh!!!!

Five days later

Subject: Hello Leo!

You obviously find a straightforward correspondence without any titillating subtexts a little too dreary, am I right?

Two days later

Subject: Hello Emmi!

That's where you're wrong, Emmi dear. Now that I know your world won't come to an end if I don't write to you, I'm not online so much. This is the reason for the long pauses. I beg your forgiveness, and for a little patience, too.

Three minutes later

Re:

Don't tell me the only reason you wrote to me for two whole years was to stop my world coming to an end?

Eight minutes later

Re:

I'm astonished that I've managed to survive another entire week without your staggering attempts to turn an argument on its head, my love!

And I'm going to answer your first question with a question of my own: You're finding the dead calm a touch boring, am I right?

Four minutes later

Re:

No, Leo, you're wrong. You're monumentally wrong! I'm totally relaxed, enjoying the quiet, my inner peace, and *fettucine* with a crayfish and almond sauce. I've already put on eight kilos. (Well, 0.8 at least.) So, are you very much in love with her?

One minute later

Re: —

Why does that bother you so much, dear penfriend?

Fifty seconds later

Re:

It doesn't bother me, I'm merely interested. Am I not allowed to be interested any more in my penfriend's most basic emotional states?

Forty seconds later

Re:

What if I said, "Yes, I am very much in love with her!"?

Thirty seconds later

Re:

I'd say: "I'm delighted for you! For both of you!"

Forty seconds later

Re:

The delight wouldn't sound sincere.

Fifty seconds later

Re:

My dear friend, you don't need to waste your time worrying about whether my delight sounds sincere! So: Are you very much in love with her?

Two minutes later

Re:

Those are Emmi-ish interrogation methods, my dear! You're not going to get an answer out of me that way.

But I'd be happy to go for a coffee again sometime and discuss those things which stir us, in spite of the dead calm.

One minute later

Re:

You want to meet up?

Three minutes later

Re:

Yes, why not? We're friends.

Two minutes later

Re:

And what will you say to "Pam"?

Fifty seconds later

Re:

Nothing at all.

Thirty seconds later

Re:

Why not?

Fifty seconds later

Re:

Because she doesn't know anything about us, as you know.

One minute later

Re:

I do indeed. But what is there not to know now? What mustn't she know? That we're penfriends?

Two minutes later

Re:

That there's a woman who asks me questions like that, and I answer them.

Fifty seconds later

Re:

But you're not answering them.

One and a half minutes later

Re:

Emmi, why do you think I've been sitting here at my computer for more than half an hour?

Thirty seconds later

Re:

Good question. Why have you?

Fifty seconds later

Re:

To correspond with you.

One minute later

Re:

True. "Pam" wouldn't understand. She'd say: "Why don't you just phone each other? You could save so much time."

Forty seconds later

Re:

True. And if you said things like that I could hang up without compunction.

Fifty seconds later

Re:

True. E-mails are more forbearing than telephones. Luckily!

Forty seconds later

True. And with e-mail you're also spending time together between messages.

Thirty seconds later

Re:

True. That's the danger.

Forty seconds later

Re:

True. And the addictive part as well.

Fifty seconds

Re:

True. Fortunately my rehab's going well. On that note:
Goodbye for today, my dear correspondent. Bernhard's
cooking, and I'm going to go and look over his shoulder.

Take care!
Emmi

CHAPTER FOURTEEN

Eight days later

Re:

Hello Emmi, shall we meet for coffee?

Four hours later

Re:

Look what's just occurred to my penfriend Leo, quite spontaneously, after a week of dignified silence in the doldrums.

Three minutes later

Re:

I didn't want to keep you from cooking and looking over other people's shoulders, Emmi dear.

Two minutes later

Re:

No false reticence, Leo, please! Otherwise we'll invite you over for supper right away. "Pam" can come too, of course. Does she like crayfish?

One minute later

Re:

This new, jolly-commune humour is weird, even by your standards, dear Emmi. One more try: Shall we meet for a coffee?

Five minutes later

Re:

My dear Leo,

Why can't you just say: "I want to . . . with you"? Why do you always ask: "Shall we . . .?" Do you not know yourself whether you want to or not? Or are reserving the right not to want to either in case I don't want to?

Fifty seconds later

Re:

Dear Emmi,

I want to have coffee with you. Do you want that too? If you don't want to, then I don't want to either, because I don't want to (have a coffee) with you against your will. So, shall we?

Five minutes later

Re:

Yes, let's do that, Leo. When do you suggest, and where?

Three seconds later

Re:

Tuesday or Thursday at 3 or 4 o'clock? Do you know Café Bodinger in Dreisterngasse?

Forty seconds later

Re:

Yes, I know it. A bit dingy, isn't it?

Fifty seconds later

Re:

Depends where you want to sit. Right under the big chandelier it's as bright as daylight, just like the Café Huber.

Thirty seconds later

Re:

Is that where you want to sit, right under the big chandelier?

Forty seconds later

Re:

I don't care where I sit.

Twenty seconds later

Re:

But I do.

Forty seconds later

Re:

Where would you rather sit, Emmi, under the big chandelier or in a dingy corner?

Thirty seconds later

Re:

Depends who I'm with.

Twenty seconds later

Re:

With me.

Twenty seconds later

Re:

With you? I hadn't really thought about it, my love.

Thirty seconds later

Re:

Then do have a think about it, my love.

One minute later

Re:

O.K., I've thought about it now. I'd quite like to sit somewhere between the dingy seats and the table right underneath the big chandelier, where the light goes from dingy to bright daylight. Thursday at 4.30 p.m.?

Fifty seconds later

Re:

Thursday at 4.30 is perfect!

Five minutes later

Re:

So, what are you expecting from our first, second, third (!), fourth, fifth meeting?

Two minutes later

Re:

Even as every meeting we've had has been unlike its predecessors, I expect that this one will be too.

Fifty seconds later

Re:

Because we're friends now.

Thirty seconds later

Re:

Yes, maybe because of that, too. And because there are parts of "us" that are painstakingly intent on bringing the idea of friendship to the table.

Five minutes later

Re:

Which do you think was our best meeting, Leo?

Fifty seconds later

Re:

The last one so far, number four.

Two minutes later

Re:

You didn't need to think long about that, did you? Is it because it was the shortest? Because it had a (relatively) clear conclusion? Because we had set the course for the future? Because "Pam" was on the doorstep?

Forty seconds later

Re:

Because of your "souvenir".

Thirty seconds later

Re:

Oh. Do you remember, then?

Twenty seconds later

Re:

I don't need to remember. I couldn't ever forget it. It's always with me.

Forty seconds later

Re:

But you haven't said a word about it.

Thirty seconds later

Re:

Words wouldn't describe it.

Forty seconds later

Re:

But words have described everything about "us" until now.

Thirty seconds later

Re:

Not this. This is no place for words. That's why "it" is what it is.

Twenty seconds later

Re:

So you can still feel "it", the same as before?

Twenty seconds later

Re:

And how!

Forty seconds later

Re:

That's lovely, Leo!!! (Pause. Pause. Pause.) So now we're friends again.

Thirty seconds later

Re:

Yes, dear penfriend, you can go now. You can look over Bernhard's shoulder while he cooks. Have a nice evening.

Re:

Good, dear penfriend, and you can watch "Pam" blow-drying her hair.

Have a nice evening yourself.

Thirty seconds

Re:

She blow-dries her hair between seven and seven-thirty in the morning (except for weekends).

Fifty seconds later

Re:

I didn't ask for such precise details.

Four days later

Subject: Café Bodinger

Hello Emmi, are we still on for this afternoon?

Best regards,
Leo

One hour later

Re:

Hello Leo,

Yes, of course. It's just . . . I have a little problem, a small logistical issue has just cropped up. But no matter. No, it isn't really a problem at all. So I'm still on for this afternoon. 4.30. See you soon!

Three minutes later

Re:

Shall we . . . sorry, do you want to postpone the meeting, Emmi?

Two minutes later

Re:

No, no, not at all. Everything's fine, no, it's not really a problem. See you later, penfriend! Looking forward to it!

Forty seconds later

Re:

Me too!

The following morning

Subject: Surprise guest!

Hello Leo, he likes you!

One hour later

Re:

How nice.

Re:

Are you pissed off? I didn't have any choice, Leo. His
handicraft lesson was cancelled and he really wanted to
come along. He wanted to meet you. He wanted to see what
a man who writes e-mails to someone (no, not "someone",
his mother) for two whole years looks like. Because, you see,
he thinks what we're doing, or rather, what we're not doing
is somehow perverse. To him you were like an alien, and all
the more fascinating because of it. What was I supposed to
do? Should I have said to him: "No, Jonas, sorry, the man
from 'Outlook', that strange planet, is mine and mine
alone"?

Ten minutes later

Re:

Yes, Emmi, I'm pissed off – really pissed off, in fact! YOU
SHOULD HAVE TOLD ME you were going to bring Jonas
along! I could have prepared myself for it.

Five minutes later

Re:

But then you would have cried off. And I would have
been disappointed. But instead I was impressed by the way
you put up such a good show, and by how attentively you
listened, and how sweet you were with him. Isn't that
better? Anyhow, Jonas is very taken with you.

Three minutes later

Re:

I'm sure his father will be delighted!

Eight minutes later

Re:

Please don't underestimate Bernhard, Leo. He stopped
thinking of you as a rival a long time ago. We're quite clear
about our relationship. Finally! We're conducting what you
might call a "partnership of convenience", however
uninspiring that may sound to you. But that's how we're
living together now. And we're doing fine! Because in the
short or long term, every partnership has to be one of
convenience – anything else would be so, so, so . . .
inconvenient, from a partnership point of view, if you
get what I mean.

Two minutes later

Re:

And I'm a newly elected member in your partnership of
convenience. Would you mind some time telling me what
function I have in your arrangement of convenience? Only
when it's convenient, of course. Having been responsible
for the virtual care of the mother, should I now turn my
attentions to the son?

One minute later

Re:

My dear Leo,

Was the hour we spent with Jonas really so awful? It was
good that he set eyes on you at last, and chatted with you,
believe me. He really loved your lecture on medieval torture
methods. He wants to know more about it.

Seven minutes later

Re:

I'm delighted, Emmi. He's a nice boy. But if I'm honest, if
I'm really, really honest, I don't think you'll understand this
– no partnership-of-convenience wife with partnership-of-
convenience children would understand it – I mean, it's
absurd, it's presumptuous, arrogant, megalomaniac even,
just my quirk, it's nutty, totally aloof, out of touch, alien.
Ah well, I'll say it anyway: The fact is, I wanted to see YOU
and talk to YOU, Emmi. That's why I arranged a meeting
with YOU. With YOU, just the two of us.

Two minutes later

Re:

But we did see each other (much to my delight). And we can
make up for the fact we didn't talk another time. Are you
free sometime next week? Tuesday, Wednesday, Thursday?
Perhaps we could spend a little longer together?

Three hours later

Subject: Hello

Hello Leo,

Are you still looking at your diary?

Five minutes later

Re:

I'm off to Boston next week with Pamela.

Three minutes later

Re:

Ah! I see. O.K. Hmm. I get it! Anything serious?

One minute later

Re:

It's exactly the kind of thing I'd love to have talked to you about.

Forty seconds later

Re:

Well, don't beat about the bush, just tell me! In writing!

Ten minutes later

Subject: (no subject)

Please! (Please, please, please!)

Subject: (no subject)

O.K., don't then, be in a huff! It suits you, Leo! I love men who are in a huff. I think they're wildly erotic. They're right up there at the top of my Eros chart: men who love motor-racing, men at travel shows, men in sandals, men in beer tents, and men in a huff!

Goodnight.

The following evening

Subject: Everything-illusion

Hello Emmi,

It's not easy to explain my situation, but I'll try anyway. Let me begin with an Emmi quote: "It seems that one person cannot give another everything." You're right. Very smart. Very astute. Very sensible. With this rationale at the back of your mind you'll never be in danger of demanding too much from another person. And without this burden you can settle instead for simply contributing to their happiness. This saves energy for more difficult times. It's how people live together. It's how people get married. It's how children are brought up. It's how promises are delivered, how "partnerships of convenience" are created, consolidated, neglected, wrenched out of sleep, saved, restarted from scratch, dragged through crises, and how they pull through in the end. Major tasks! I have a great deal of respect for all that, honestly I do. Alone: I can't be, don't want to be, don't think, don't tick alone. I may be grown up and two years older than you, but I've still got IT, and I'm not (yet) prepared to abandon it, from the "everything-illusion".

The reality: "It seems that one person cannot give another everything." My illusion: "But it should be his ambition. And he should never stop trying."

Marlene never loved me. I would have been prepared to give her "everything", but she was never particularly interested in what I was offering. She accepted a fraction of it out of gratitude, or maybe it was an act of mercy, but I was allowed to keep the rest for myself. All in all it was only enough for half a dozen attempts at take-off. The landings came quickly and were extremely bumpy, especially for me.

It's different with Pamela. She loves me. She really loves me. Don't worry, Emmi, I'm not going to bore you again with details of all the things we have in common. The problem: Pamela doesn't feel happy here. She's homesick, missing her family, her friends, her colleagues, her places, her routines. She hardly lets it show, she wants to keep it secret from me, she wants to protect me because she knows it has nothing to do with me, and because she assumes that there's nothing I can do to change it.

So as a surprise I went and bought flights to Boston. She wept a year's worth of tears out of sheer joy. Since then she's been a changed woman, as if she's on some happy drug. She's seeing it as no more than a "two-week holiday", but I can't rule out the possibility that it will turn into something else further down the line. Without saying anything to her I've arranged some interviews at German studies institutes. There may be a longer-term job opportunity for me.

I have no desire to live in Boston, Emmi, not for one minute. I'd much rather stay here – for a number of different reasons, no, not different reasons, for one specific reason. But this reason is so... how would you put it? "This reason is so, so, so – without any reason." It has no foundation. It's just something that's going around in my head. No, worse than that, it's something going around in my gut.

It is probable that my future together with Pamela, should there be one, lies several thousand kilometres away from here. I think I find it easier than she does to change, to adapt to new surroundings.

Her happiness spurs me on. I'd like to continue seeing her as I have over the past few days. And I want her to continue seeing me as she has for several days. She looks on me as a man who is capable of giving her "everything". No, it's not that I'm capable of doing it, but I'm prepared to. In between the two is illusion. I'd like to hold on to it for a while longer. Why bother living, if not for "everything-illusions"?

Two hours later

Re:

"She loves me. She really loves me." "I want to give her everything." "I think I find it easier than she does to change, to adapt to new surroundings." "Her happiness spurs me on." "If only she could continue seeing me as she has for several days!"...

Leo, Leo, Leo! For you, love is ... sitting at the controls of someone else's happiness. BUT WHERE ARE YOU? What about your own happiness? What about your desires? Don't you have any of your own? Do you just have "Pam"'s? Is that all you have, feelings in your gut? – I feel so sorry for you. No, I feel sorry for myself. No I don't, I feel sorry for both of us. Tonight's a sad night, somehow. A dark evening in late spring. Dead calm. The doldrums. I'm going to have a whisky. And then I'll decide whether or not to have another. Because I've got my own desires to be looking after. And I'm looking for MY happiness. Fortunately. Or unfortunately. No idea. You're a lovely man, Leo! You really are! But can you only be loved, or can you also love someone yourself?

Goodnight,
Emmi

Two days later

Subject: Four questions

1.) How are you?

2.) When are you leaving?

3.) Are you going to write again before you go?

Three minutes later

Re:

That was only three!

Thirty seconds later

Re:

I know. I just wanted to check that you were still on this planet and able to count.

Eight minutes later

Re:

Re: 1.)   I don't feel all that great. Something else is going around in my gut: an intestinal infection. Whenever I'm about to go away *à deux* I always get ill. It was like that with Marlene.

Re: 2.)   We're off tomorrow afternoon (so long as I can fit a loo into my hand luggage).

Re: 3.)   Will I write again? Emmi, your dark-evening-in-late-spring e-mail made me quite depressed. I didn't know how to reply. There's no illustrated instruction manual for sighting and salvaging happiness. Everybody seeks their own happiness in their own way, and in those places where they believe they will find it the fastest. But maybe it was too much to expect some encouraging words from you about "Operation Boston".

Half an hour later

Re:

You're right, Leo. I'm sorry, but for me "Boston" is hopelessly loaded with negative connotations, I couldn't think of anything encouraging to say. You have to understand that I think your willingness to give a woman "everything" is remarkable, courageous, fascinating. (I was also going to write "noble" and "gentlemanly", but thought better of it.) I wish you all the very best with that, the best possible luck. Leaving the illustrated instruction manual aside, everybody defines happiness in their own way.

I think more about my own; you seem to think more about "Pam"'s. I hope you factor yourself in somewhere as well.

Oh, by the way, my therapist thinks it's perfectly O.K. if I let you know, for your trip, that I look forward to your return, I mean, in two weeks' time. She thought it would be fine for me to admit that I'll sort of be waiting for you to come back, because I think it somehow so, so, so – lovely that you'll be back, when you *do* come back, that is. Just lovely. Do you understand? And try eating rice cakes, not bananas. Bananas don't help at all. Bananas are the greatest myth in the entire history of diarrhoea-related illnesses.

Take care, my love!

Five minutes later

Re:

What about the fourth question?

Two minutes later

Re:

Ah yes, the fourth question!

4) When you come back, could the four of us meet up one time? Fiona would really like to meet you. Jonas told her you look like Kevin Spacey, but with even less hair. Fiona loves Kevin Spacey, even without hair, although I think his hair could be considered one of his more interesting features. Anyway, I think Jonas might be confusing Spacey with that ghastly sit-com actor, the one with the long face, what's his name? Doesn't matter. Shall we meet up again soon, Leo? Say yes!

One minute later

Subject: SAY YES!

See subject above and do it!

Fifty seconds later

Re:

Yes! Yes! Yes! Forgive me, I was on the loo. And the next sentence can't be too long or I'll have to break it off midflow. Bye for now, my love!

CHAPTER FIFTEEN

Eight days later

Subject: Home is "you"

Dear Emmi

I've been in Boston's clutches for a week now. When this city gets a grip on you it never lets go. In the area where we're staying Pamela knows one in every five families, and one in every two of these invites us to lunch or dinner. That means we go to eat with acquaintances around eight times a day. And this doesn't include the visits to relatives. It might sound terribly quaint to you. But I'm enjoying it, the friendliness of these people is infectious, from morning to night I see open, laughing, beaming faces. It rubs off on me. You know how I have a rather peculiar approach to happiness. Generally it comes from outside, rarely from within me. Rarely, but it does happen. I love thinking about you, Emmi! I have to give that sentence more emphasis: I LOVE THINKING ABOUT YOU, EMMI! I was absolutely terrified that the painful yearnings from my Boston days for refuges and hiding places would be reawakened. I'm so grateful to you for not having bolted the door through which I once vanished, abandoning our "us". Even at so great a distance I can now be "at home" without heartache. Home is where you are, Emmi. I'm looking forward to being geographically closer to you again. I'm looking forward to our next meeting. By all means bring along some of your adolescent children as a surprise. And at some point I'll tell you a thing or two about you and "it" and me. And now we've been invited to dinner at Maggy Wellington's, a friend of Pamela's from university.

Take care,
Your penfriend,
Leo

Four days later

Subject: Arrived?

Dear Emmi,

A few days ago I sent you an e-mail from here in Boston. I don't know whether you got it; I received an error message. I'll summarize the contents in a couple of sentences: 1.) I'm fine, but/and I'm missing you! 2.) I'm looking forward to our next meeting!

See you soon,
Your penfriend,
Leo

Three days later

Subject: Arrived?

Hi Leo,

Did your plane land safely? Are you back home in flat 15? Thank you for your lovely message from the U.S.! I'll now summarize your two East-Coast messages. 1.) Home is wherever your penfriend Emmi is. 2.) Boston is a place full of happy faces, a place where you can make "Pam" happy on the inside (and yourself happy on the outside at the same time). Question: do you now know where you'll end up? And the time frame?

Warm greetings,
Emmi

P.S. Oh yes: tell me something about "you and 'it' and me"!

The following morning
Subject: Stuck?

Or have you decided to stay in Boston indefinitely?

Seven hours later
Subject: (no subject)
Dear Emmi,

I made a big mistake yesterday. I told Pamela about you. I'll be in touch again as soon as I can. Please don't wait!
Love,
Leo

Ten minutes later
Re:

Oh, Leo!!! Why do you always do rational things at the most irrational times? O.K., I won't wait.

Lots of love,
Emmi

One day later
Subject: (no subject)
No, I won't wait.

One day later
Subject: (no subject)
As I said, I won't wait.

One day later
Subject: (no subject)
I'm not waiting, I'm not waiting, I'm not waiting.

One day later
Subject: (no subject)
I'm not waiting, I'm not waiting, I'm not waiting, I'm not
waiting, I'm not waiting.

One day later
Subject: Finished!
I'm sick of not waiting! Now I am waiting!

Six hours later

Subject: Leeeo?

Don't you want to write to me any more, or can't you write, or aren't you allowed to write? What did you tell her about me? WHAT? WHAT? WHAT? If you defined your happiness with even the slightest reference to mine, Leo, then you'd feel it: you're making me deeply unhappy at the moment. Please operate the controls. And do me a favour, for God's sake, end this silence!

Yours bitterly,
Emmi

One hour later

Subject: Accountant!

You've given me no choice, Leo: I'm going to count to ten and then I'm phoning my accountant to arrange an appointment for tomorrow. You know what that means, don't you? And when it comes to sorting out personal matters, my American-English is perfect. One. Two. Three...

The following morning

Subject: Ultimatum

Hi Leo,

My therapist thinks I should write you one final e-mail, and I should tell you that it really will be the very last unless you answer me soon – or sooner than soon, right now, in fact – and even if you do, it really will be the last e-mail. I guarantee it! And she also thinks I should suggest that we meet to talk everything through properly. I'm to tell you in no uncertain terms that I definitely don't want "Pam" to know anything about this meeting, nor should she find out about it afterwards, because this is about us, and not about anyone else. Do you think my therapist has expressed herself clearly enough?

In anticipation of your immediately forthcoming response,
Emmi

Three hours later

Re:

Dear Emmi,

Please give me some time. She's completely bewildered and has retreated back into her shell. I have to try to win back her trust and establish a basis for dialogue. Your psychotherapist would surely agree that I need to come clean with her before the two of us – you and I – meet. My battle with Pamela is not yet over; maybe it hasn't even really broken out yet. She finally has to have a chance to talk, she has to let it out, she has to tell me to my face what it is that is hurting her so terribly, what is making her suffer, what it is that she has to reproach me for. I'm standing at the entrance to a dark tunnel, and I need to walk down it with her. You can't come with us; you have to stay out in the open. But when I reach the other end, I'll tell you everything, everything about you and me. I promise! Dear Emmi, please have patience and don't be lost to me! I feel more miserable than I have in a long time.

One hour later

Re:

I won't be lost to you, dear Leo. But YOU will be lost to me. You'll walk along the dark tunnel with "Pam", and at the end of it you'll emerge into Boston's bright sunshine. Don't worry, I'm sure you'll "come clean" with her, but that can mean only one thing: no more contact between you and me. It's your one chance to keep up your faltering "everything-illusion". I have absolutely no idea what you've told her about the two of us. You obviously haven't said that we're old friends, or casual acquaintances who write to each other once in a while. If I were "Pam" and I knew even the smallest piece of the whole truth of our story, I'd get hold of a megaphone and scream into your ear at one-minute intervals: "No more Emma, never again!" But she's probably more inhibited, more prudent, and much more polite. She'll just think it instead. But that won't change the logical outcome: finishing with Emmi. "Pam" will demand that of you. And I completely understand why! And you'll do it. I know you.

So now you have all the time in the world to "come clean", Leo. First with her, and then with me. And then maybe at some point you can come clean with yourself too. That's what I hope for you, more than anything.

Much love,
Emmi

213

Three days later

Subject: Spiderman

Hi Leo,

Jonas sends his regards. He wants to go and see "Spiderman III" with you (and with me, if I really have to). If you have a tendency to vertigo, he'd be quite happy with "Return of the Jedi". His father is away for three weeks, on tour in Asia. Playing to packed concert halls every day. And if a concert hall is full in Asia, you can bet it's about five times as full as it would be here.

Actually, I just wanted to let you know that I'm not yet lost to you, as promised.

Much love
Emmi

Ten minutes later

Re:

Thanks, Emmi!!!

One minute later

Re:

You see, Leo, that's all I needed to hear! All you have to do is write to me once a week – "Thanks, Emmi", and don't forget the three exclamation marks – and I'd quite happily manage another few years at my end of the tunnel.

Four days later

Subject: Warm

Warm today, isn't it?

(If you don't have the time or the strength to think up your own answer, I recommend: "Yes, very warm!!!" or "Drink lots of water!!!" Don't forget the exclamation marks!!!)

Seven hours later

Subject: (no subject)

Shame. I was really expecting an answer this time.

The following evening

Subject: A little light

Is it still so dark in that tunnel? Or can you by now see a little light at the end? Is it glowing? Then it's me. (Sunburn.)

The following morning

Subject: What, exactly?

Dear Leo,

What, exactly, did you tell "Pam" about the two of us? Did you tell her any of the tricky bits? For example:

a.) That we've had an e-mail relationship for the past two and a half years?

b.) That you fled to Boston to protect my marriage?

c.) That we found each other online again after you came home, and that we've met offline five times?

d.) That we even had sex once?

e.) If the answer to d.) is yes, did you tell her the circumstances in which d.) happened, and how you found d.)?

f.) That we met for a few minutes the night before she came to live here?

g.) What I gave you that time as a "souvenir"?

And have the following factors enabled you to come out of it relatively unscathed? For example:

h.) That our relationship is from now on to be described as "profound, platonic, amicable".

i.) That our correspondence should not interfere with your long-term relationship in any way.

j.) That I do not diminish your relationship with her, nor hers with you.

k.) Because in any case I've moved back in with my family, in order to continue my unprecedented and entirely rational "partnership of convenience" after a well-earned breather.

l.) And because the two of you are going to be emigrating to Boston in the foreseeable future anyway.

Five minutes later

Re:

a.), b.), c.), d.), e.), f.), h.), i.), j.), k.), l.).

One minute later

Re:

Everything? The whole lot? The entire catalogue? Are you crazy, Leo? If I were her, the only reason for not dispatching you into outer space would be because then I couldn't extract the hairs from your chin, one by one. You'd be too far away.

Thirty seconds later

Re:

And I knew that we'd be able to have a good chat about it all.

Forty seconds later

Re:

Hey, Leo, I've only just noticed: everything apart from g.). You left g.) out. You confessed to "Pam" that you and I indulged in a sexual act. You even told her what you felt at the time (or rather, what you felt differently or didn't feel at all). But you haven't told her what I gave you as a souvenir? Why not?

One minute later

Re:

Because if only one thing had to remain just between you and me, it was my greatest and most beautiful secret.

Two minutes later

Re:

That was nicely put, Leo, even if I had to read the sentence twice! Or as you might say in your shorthand: Thanks, Leo!!!

Six days later

Subject: Lost to me?

Dear Emmi,

Are you lost to me? I couldn't blame you if you were.

One day later

Subject: When?

You're the silent one of the two of us, Leo! So tell me, when are you emigrating to Boston?

Five minutes later

Re:

Please, Emmi, be patient with me for a few days more. In a week's time I'll tell you everything. EVERYTHING!

Seven minutes later

Re:

Can you tell me EVERYTHING in a week's time? Or do you have to tell me EVERYTHING in a week's time? Can Pam know that you're going to tell me EVERYTHING in a week's time? Or is Pam in fact demanding that you tell me EVERYTHING in a week's time? And why a week? What's going to happen over the course of this week? O.K., I get it, I'm only going to find out in a week's time.

Bye bye!

Be in touch in a week, then.

Four minutes later

Subject: Istria

Oh, by the way, Bernhard gets back from Japan in a week and two days. In a week and four days we're going with the kids to Istria for our summer holidays. In case you're thinking of meeting before then to tell me EVERYTHING, then let's make a date as soon as possible!

All the best for a successful week,
Emmi

Six days later

Subject: Time's nearly up

Hi Leo,

Tomorrow your week will be up. So how is EVERYTHING? Where is EVERYTHING? What is EVERYTHING?

Subject: Everything (is over)

Dear Emmi,

Pamela and I have split up. She's flying to Boston on Monday, alone. That is EVERYTHING.

Re:

Dear Leo,

That's quite a lot, I have to say. But it can't be EVERYTHING. It can't HAVE BEEN everything, just like that. I don't believe you. Come on, Leo! Do you want to meet? Do you want to get it off your chest and have a good cry? I can be there for you right now, round the clock, so to speak, for the next two days. If you want to meet, then let's meet! If you're not sure whether we should meet, we should meet! If you don't know whether you want to meet anyone at all, then meet me! But if you're certain you don't know whether it would be a good thing or not for you to meet me – because how could you know? – then don't meet me. No, do actually, even then! So there. Full stop. I didn't want to be discreet with my offer. I don't think I could be any less discreet. And I won't ever offer myself so indiscreetly again. And that's a promise!

220

Re:

Dear Emmi,

In a few hours I'll be on the train to Hamburg. I'm going to
visit my sister Adrienne and I'll stay with her until Tuesday.
You're off with your family to Croatia on Wednesday, aren't
you? So we probably won't see each other until after that.
Emmi, I know you're dying to know what happened. You
have every right to know. And I feel I need to tell you.
Really I do! You'll find out in all its facets, I guarantee it.
Let's just have our time in Hamburg and Croatia first. I need
to see things more clearly. I need distance – from Pamela and
from myself. Not from you, Emmi, believe me, not from you!

Eight minutes later

Re:

You know, you couldn't be more distant than you already
are, my love. You're driving me crazy with your endless
delays, denials, empty promises and almost monosyllabic
about-turns! When I get back from Istria, I expect you'll be
announcing your engagement to "Pam". But sadly you won't
be able to share any "facet" of your decision with me.
Because you'll have to "see things more clearly first". I don't
want this any more, Leo! You mustn't be cross: whatever it is
making you wait this time before telling me something
profound about yourself, I'm waiting with you. I've been
waiting ever since I've known you. Over the past two and a
half years I've waited three times as much as I have in the
preceding thirty-three. If only I'd known what I was waiting
for! I'm sick to death of waiting. Basically I'm all waited out.

Sorry! (And now you're going to go all silent and sulky on me again.)

One minute later

Re:

No, Emmi. I won't go silent and I won't go sulky. I'm going to Hamburg. And I'm coming back. And I'll write to you. And I won't announce any engagements.

Lots of love,
Leo

CHAPTER SIXTEEN

Five days later

Subject: Adieu Pamela

Good morning, dear Emmi,

Greetings to the Mediterranean from flat 15! I'm back. I'm myself again. I'm sitting on the terrace with my laptop. At my back is one of those men's flats that looks pitifully bare after a woman has just left.

I spoke to her on the phone yesterday. She arrived O.K. It's raining in Boston. I find it astonishing that we can already talk to each other again; a bit awkward, maybe – dry mouths, difficulty swallowing, choking noises, grinding teeth – but we can do it. It was only a week ago that we managed to ditch each other at the same time, without any advance warning, without giving any reasons. I started it off: "Pamela, I think we should . . ." and Pamela completed it, ". . . end it, you're right!"

We're both to blame, we failed together. It was smooth, elegant, perfectly choreographed with very high technical merit, "synchronized". We gathered our disappointments, threw them into a heap and shared them out fairly. Each of us took our allocated half. That's how we parted. When we said farewell we hugged, kissed and gave each other a friendly punch on the shoulder. And that's how, without saying a word, each of us extended our "warmest sympathy" to the other. We cried when we saw each other's tears. It was like being at a funeral, as if we'd lost a relative we had in common. And in fact we have! It's just that we knew them by different names. Pamela's was Trust, mine Illusion. (To be continued – I'm going to send this now and make myself a coffee. Won't be long!)

Ten seconds later

Subject: Out-of-office autoreply

I am on holiday and will respond to my e-mails on 23 July.

With best wishes,
Emmi Rothner

Thirty minutes later

Re:

I had expected that, Emmi. And actually it's a good thing! You see, I've no idea whether you want to listen to all this. Now the earliest I'll find out is in a week and a half. So, I'll just keep on shamelessly recapping, my love:

Pamela was the first woman who did not remind me of you, who I didn't compare to you, who had nothing of you – my virtual fantasy – and yet who I found attractive. When I saw her I knew instantly that I had to fall in love with her. This was the fallacy, the mistake: the "had to", the plan, the intention, my insistent efforts. I was driven by the idea of loving her. I was consumed by it. Until the very end I did everything for it. Apart from one thing: I never questioned whether I was actually in love with her.

There were three phases with Pamela. Four months in Boston – that was my best time with her, it was MY time with her; I wouldn't have missed a single day of it. When I came home from America last summer, you were there, Emmi. Again, still: YOU! My feelings carefully closeted away. How naive I was to believe that they could disperse of their own accord. You were quick to remind me that there could be no end without a beginning. We met up. I saw you. SAW YOU! What should I said on that occasion? What should I say about it now? I was in phase two with Pamela: a long-distance relationship, broken up by thrilling voyages of discovery and intense pangs of desire for a perfectly normal and more permanent state of togetherness – going out to buy bread and milk, changing the hoover bags. How did I while away the time waiting for my future? With you, Emmi. Who did I lie with virtually? You, Emmi. Who did I live with in my secret inner world? You, Emmi. Only ever with you. And now my most wonderful fantasies had a face, too. Your face.

Then Pamela came and moved in. Phase three. I flicked the master switch in my head: Emmi off, Pamela on. A brutal undertaking. Total focus on the "woman for life", the chosen one, the one I had to love. "Everything-illusion" applied in practice. You gave me the cue; I thought I could make a better fist of it than you and Bernhard with your "marriage of convenience". Maybe I just wanted to prove to you that I could. I was determined to do everything to make Pamela happy. At the beginning she felt flattered and secure. I felt good, too. It was a diversionary tactic, a helpful course of occupational therapy – all I had to do was to make sure I didn't listen to my inner voice, didn't have too much Emmi-time. Every personal e-mail, every intimate thought of you had to be immediately exonerated and compensated for with a confirmation of my bond to Pamela. That's how I soothed my bad conscience. Well, she wasn't impressed for very long by my excessive declarations of love. Soon she felt irritated, overwhelmed, cornered. She needed space, an outlet, a refuge where she had home advantage. There was only one place for that: Boston. I saw it as the only opportunity to realize my illusion.

You've read my e-mails. Our taster-holiday was good enough to persuade me that I wanted to make a go of it with her on the East Coast. We'd planned to "emigrate" at the beginning of next year, things had been put in place, the prospect of a job and a flat. But then, but then, but then . . . Yes, then I told her about you, Emmi.

Happy beach time!
Leo

Eight hours later

Re:

But why did you tell her about me?

Hi Leo, by the way. I hope you didn't seriously believe that I'd let you reel off your melodramatic "Pam"-phase analyses for an entire week without putting my own gloss on it. I'm not going to have you run out of steam and then go silent again for months. Talking of hot air, right now I'm in a delightful, crypt-like, low-lit internet café, about three metres square, with black walls. It must be the hangout of the pierced successors to Croatia's No Future movement, the kind of place where in five minutes you inhale more as a passive smoker than your average chain smoker would in an hour. From where I'm sitting in this nihilistic fug, your reflections on "Pam" seem all the more bizarre. So come on, tell me, don't be shy! Why did you tell her about me? What happened then? And what will happen now? I'll be back in this fine internet establishment sometime over the next few days to collect your notes on the subject, if my lungs aren't scorched in the meantime.

Kiss kiss
Emmi

P.S. (how original!) I look forward to seeing you again!

One day later

Subject: Point of contact

Dear Emmi,

How lovely to get you on such ravishing form! The Croatian sea and crypt air is clearly doing your sensitive arteries the world of good.

1.) Why did I tell Pam, Pamela about you? I had to. I came to the point where I had no choice. It was YOUR point, Emmi! Once described and identified by me thus: "on the palm of my left hand, roughly in the middle, where the life line is crossed by deep creases and turns down towards the artery". It's the place where you accidentally touched me on our second meeting. It has remained my ultimate Emmi point of contact, preserved for all eternity.

Months later, at our notorious five-minute meeting before Pamela got here, you gave me your "souvenir", your

"present". Were you aware of the significance of this
gesture? Did you have any idea what it would lead to?
"Psst!" you whispered. "Don't say anything, Leo! Not a
word!" You took my left hand, brought it up to your mouth,
and kissed our point of contact. And you gently stroked
your thumb over it, too. Your parting words: "Bye, Leo.
All the best. Don't forget me!" And then the door was
closed. I've played this scene back hundreds of times,
recreated your kiss on the point thousands of times. Given
that I'm not exactly skilled in describing the various stages
of sexual arousal, I'll leave it to you to imagine how I felt.

In any case, from then on I found it impossible to be
intimate with Pamela without feeling your point and
without thinking of you and feeling you, Emmi. And so that
theory about cheating I'd so pompously elaborated was shot
to pieces. Can you remember the words I wrote to you? "My
feelings for you don't detract from those I have for her. The
two have nothing to do with each other. They aren't in
competition." Rubbish! Inexcusable! Totally unrealistic.
Disproved by a single, tiny point. For a long time I didn't
want to admit that my left hand was beginning to avoid
Pamela's body. I didn't want to acknowledge the defensive
position it adopted, how intent it was on protecting its
secret, hiding it in a clenched fist.

In the end Pamela must have noticed. That evening she made
a forceful grab for my unwilling left hand, tried everything
she could to prise open my clenched fist, turned it into a
game, gave a strained laugh, increased the pressure, kneeled
on my forearm. To start with I put up some serious
resistance. But finally I realized I wasn't going to be able to
hide our "everything" within my five fingers forever. I
jerked my hand out of her grasp, opened my fist, held my

hand up to her face and said in exasperation (I felt terrible, totally at her mercy, humiliated, resentful, condemned), "Here you are! Have it! Happy now?" She was distraught, asked me what was wrong all of a sudden, whether it was something she'd said or done. I just apologized. Pamela had no idea why. But afterwards I had no choice: I told her about you.

Actually, all I wanted to do at first was to say your name and see how I got on. I used the story of the indomitable seventh wave as an opportunity to mention that I'd just recently been reminded of it – "by Emmi, a good friend". Pamela immediately pricked up her ears and asked, "Emmi? Who's she? Where do you know her from?" The floodgates were now open, and I spent a good hour spouting forth about us until every last drop had trickled out. In fact it was the perfect example of those soaring, foaming, tumbling seventh waves you described. A wave that broke free, changing everything, recreating the landscape, leaving nothing the same as before.

Enjoy a lovely morning in the sea!
Leo

Three hours later

Subject: Adieu

2.) What happened after that? Not much. The tide ebbed. A lull. Silence. Embarrassment. A shaking of heads. Mistrust. Cold. Quivering. Shivering. Her first question: "Why are you telling me all this?" Me: "I thought it was about time you knew." Her: "Why?" Me: "Because it was part of my life." Her: "It?" Me: "Emmi." Her: "Was?" Me:

"We became friends, we send each other e-mails occasionally. She's happily back together with her husband." Her: "And if she weren't?" Me: "She is." Her: "Do you still love her?" Me: "Pamela, I love you! I'm moving to Boston with you. Isn't that proof enough?" She smiled and gave the back of my head a fleeting stroke. I could work out what she was thinking.

Then she stood up and went to the door. She turned again and said, "Just one more question: Am I here just because of her?" I hesitated, I thought about it, I said, "Pamela, there's a background to everything. Nothing exists in a vacuum." At this she left the room. For her the subject was closed. I made several attempts to talk to her about it. I longed for a discussion, I would have put up with a violent hailstorm just so that another clear day could finally dawn. To no avail. Pamela thwarted any talk. There was no argument, no reproach, no nasty words, not even a nasty look. No, there were no looks at all, only glancing blows. Her voice sounded like a recording. The softer her touches, the more painful they seemed. We continued as if nothing had happened. We tortured each other like this for some weeks, together, side by side, in concert, in sync. Until finally I understood: I hadn't only told Pamela the history of you and me. I had also told her our whole story, hers and mine. And I had told it all the way to the end. There was nothing left but for us to say adieu.

The following morning

Subject: So, so, so sad!

Hi Leo,

I'd love to be able to distract us both from the contents of your e-mail with some kind daft joke. But this time I can't do it. I hate stories with unhappy endings, especially so early in the morning. Yours has brought tears to my eyes, and now I can't stop crying. The man sitting next to me, forsaken by the night and looking as if he has a dental brace embedded in his forehead, he even stubbed out his half-smoked cigarette in sympathy. I find everything you've written so, so, so desperately sad, Leo, and the way in which you've written it is sad too! I feel so, so, so sorry for you! I would so, so, so much like to embrace you now and never let you go. You are so, so, so sweet! And so, so, so unbelievably lacking in any talent for affairs of the heart. You do everything at exactly the wrong moment, and if it were ever the right time to do something, you certainly wouldn't do it, or you'd do it wrong. You and "Pam" – it could never have come to anything. I knew that the moment I set eyes on her. Playing golf together, fine. Visiting relatives in Boston, eating turkey at Christmas, sex once in a while (if you must), all that I can understand. But I couldn't see you living together!

Right, now I've got to calm myself down. Fiona's waiting outside. She wants us to try and find a shopping mall in the local fishing village . . . Time for your next tragic chapter.

Until soon, my love
Emmi

Subject: Part three

3.) So where does the story go from here? – I don't have a clue, Emmi dear. I'm still jotting down a few key words to plan my next six months. If you have any useful tips, then please send them over. I might spend the remainder of the summer in Hamburg with my sister and wait by the North Sea for a groundbreaking seventh wave. Anyway, there's no reason for you to feel sad or worry about me. Even if I feel a little worn down, I really am happy. I can't see much, but what I *can* see, I see clearly. You, for example, in the Croatian crypt-café and on the beach, in a green bikini (please don't disappoint me by saying it's blue!).

If my maths is right, you and your family have five days' holiday left. I hope you can enjoy them undisturbed. I'll do my bit to help by burying myself in my stacks of neglected seminar work, and won't write to you again until you're back. Thanks, anyway, for – your ears, your eyes, for your point of contact. For you! You're so terribly important to me. You really, really are!

Leo.

Three hours later

Re:

As it happens I do have a useful tip for you, Leo. Would you add it to your list of key words, please? – A week on Thursday, time: 7.30 p.m., place: Ristorante Impressione, a table for two booked in the name of Emmi Rothner. I look forward to it! Please make sure you're there, however worn away you're feeling! Please, please, please!

A kiss from the crypt,
Emmi

P.S. You were close: it was the brown and white bikini. I'm
going to wear the green one today. And then when you see
me, you'll see me *really* clearly!

Three days later

Re: Impressione

Hi Leo,

You haven't yet said whether you can come on Thursday.
I don't want to force you, I just want to know why I'm
plonking myself down in the sun for an hour every day,
surrounded by people in loungers. Until a week ago I used
to pity them for indulging in this dull non-activity that
turns your brain to mush.

Lots of love
Emmi

P.S. Jonas "Spiderman" Rothner sends his regards! He made
a bet with me that you were a passionate hang-glider and
windsurfer. I put my money on you being a beachcomber,
mussel picker and stone collector.

One day later

Subject: Admission

Dear Emmi,

I didn't want to burden you with this on your holiday, but I
have to admit that I'm scared about our meeting.

Four hours later

Re:

Oh, Leo, you don't have to be scared. It'll be the sixth time we've met. The seventh is the one you'll have to watch out for. ☺

By the way, I'm hereby modifying my personal chart of the most erotic men on earth: racing-car enthusiasts, travel show visitors, men in sandals, men in beer tents, sulky men and — men who are scared.

Until soon,
Emmi.

Three minutes later

Re:

Dear Emmi,

What are you expecting from our "Italian evening"? I know you'll be familiar with the question, but I find it gets in the way of every meeting, particularly this one.

Two minutes later

Re:

1.) Antipasti di pesce

2.) Linguine al limone

3.) Panna cotta

4.) And to go with all that, before it, after it, during it and accompanied by wine: Leo!

5.) Sitting opposite me, there to talk to, to hear his voice, to
look at him with my own eyes, close enough to touch,
kneecap to kneecap almost: Leo!

(If you promise to write back straightaway without thinking
too hard about it, however much that goes against your
natural instincts, I'll hang about in this smoke-box for a few
more minutes.)

One minute later

Re:

Are you going to behave differently from before?

Thirty seconds later

Re:

You can't ask questions like that, Leo. Who can tell? And
anyway, every time we see each other it's different.

Forty seconds later

Re:

I mean because of Pamela.

Two minutes later

Re:

I know exactly what you mean. And I don't think I would
behave differently towards you because of "Pam". If I
behave differently, it's because of you. Or me. Or put
another way: if you behave differently towards me, then I'll

behave differently towards you. And because up until now you've always behaved differently towards me, you'll behave differently this time too, and in turn I'll behave differently towards you. And besides, we've never been out for dinner together. The very fact of your eating will mean that you're behaving differently towards me. And my reaction to that will be to eat back, that's a promise! Do you mind if I climb back out of this crypt into the sunshine?

Three minutes later

Subject: May I?

Does that mean I'm allowed back into the sunshine? O.K., I'm off. Bye, Leo. I'll be in touch when I'm home.

Kiss, kiss,
Emmi.

Simultaneously

Re:

Of course you are. See you soon. Please write when you're back. Much love.

Yours,
Leo

Three hours later

Subject: Nice bikini

I like the bikini. I like you in green!

One day later

Re:

Aren't you the daring one!

Two days later

Subject: Me first

Hello Emmi,

A warm welcome home! Please delete me from your "chart of erotic men". I'm looking forward to tomorrow evening, 7.30, at the Italian. I'm free from all care. I'm not worried in the slightest that our meeting might go pear-shaped (unless you want to change your pudding order).

Leo

Three hours later

Re:

The new Leo: quick as lightning, fearless, famished, ready for anything!

(Thank you for your warm welcome. And I'M looking forward to it more than you!)

Four minutes later

Re:

The old Emmi: clearly back home in fine fettle!

(Thanks for "I'M" and "more"!)

The following morning

Subject: Still in good shape?

Dear Emmi,

Are we still on for this evening?

Thirty minutes later

Re:

Yes, of course we are, Leo my love. Oh, I almost forgot to tell you. Bernhard and the kids are coming too. Is that alright?

Ten minutes later

Subject: Joke!

That was a joke, Leo! A JOKE! A *JO-OKE*!

Three minutes later

Re:

I can see it's going to be a fun evening! I'd rather not send any more e-mails now.

See you later,
Leo

One minute later

Re:

Looking forward to seeing you!

Thirty seconds later

Re:

And me you!

CHAPTER SEVENTEEN

The following morning

Subject: (no subject)

Good sleep?

Five minutes later

Re:

Didn't even get to sleep. Too many images in my head, too obsessed with looking at them over and over again. How do you feel, my love?

One minute later

Re:

I can only hope you feel the same as I do, my love.

Two minutes later

Re:

If you were to double the intensity of your feelings, then you'd feel roughly as I do, Emmi.

Three minutes later

Re:

Halve that and multiply by four, that's about how I feel! Why didn't you ask me to come up to your place?

Fifty seconds later

Re:

Because you would have said no, amongst other things, Emmi.

Forty seconds later

Re:

Really, would I? Did I look as though I would have said no?

One minute later

Re:

People who say no seldom look as if they'd say no before they say it. Otherwise no-one would ever ask them.

Forty seconds later

Re:

Says Leo, the great understander of women, drawing from
his vast and pertinent experience of such matters. And after
one hundred nos, even though the women in question
hadn't looked as if they'd say no at all, he's simply stopped
asking the question.

Thirty seconds later

Re:

You would have said no, Emmi. Am I right?

Forty seconds later

Re:

And you wouldn't have had any objections if I'd come up to
yours? Am I right, Leo?

Thirty seconds later

Re:

What makes you think that?

Forty seconds later

Re:

Someone who kisses and . . . erm . . . "hugs" like that would
not have any objections.

Fifty seconds later

Re:

So concludes Emmi, man-conqueror, on the basis of innumerable taste and touch tests.

Forty seconds later

Re:

So did you want me to come up to the flat, or not?

Twenty seconds later

Re:

Of course I did.

Thirty seconds later

Re:

Well then why didn't you ask me? I would have said yes. Really!

Thirty seconds later

Re:

Really? Shit!

Fifty seconds later

Re:

But the doorstep episode wasn't bad either, my love. I've experienced a fair few smooching-on-the-doorstep episodes in my time. (O.K., most of them were on the big screen.) Very few indeed have been as good and as long-lasting as that one. There wasn't a single boring bit. I felt as if I was seventeen all over again.

Forty seconds later

Re:

It was an overwhelming evening, Emmi!

Fifty seconds later

Re:

Yes, overwhelming, that's for sure! There's just one thing I don't understand, my love.

Thirty seconds later

Re:

What's that, my love?

Twenty seconds later

Re:

How could you? How could you? How could you?

Thirty seconds later

Re:

Out with it!

Forty seconds later

Re:

Leo, how could you leave four of those seven sensational *tortelloni asparagi e prosciutto in salsa limone* on your plate?

Fifty seconds later

Re:

I did it for you!

Thirty seconds later

Re:

You get extra points for that.

Fifty seconds later

Re:

So, Emmi love. I'm going to shut down now, close my eyes, freeze time, and dream – of it and of more besides.

Kiss!

Forty seconds later

Re:

Sleep well, my sweet! This evening I'll write whatever else I wanted to say. I return your kiss! No, I don't return it. You can have one of your own. I'm keeping the one you've given me. You don't get kisses like that every day.

Nine hours later

Subject: Something I noticed

Dear Leo,

Are you awake? I just wanted to point out that you didn't mention Bernhard once yesterday evening.

Forty seconds later

Re:

Nor did you, Emmi.

Fifty seconds later

Re:

I can keep myself under control on that front. But I'm not used to it coming from you, my love.

Eight minutes later

Re:

You may have to (or I may let you) get used to it, my love. I can learn sometimes, too: Bernhard is your concern, not mine. He's your husband, not mine. When you kiss me it's your conscience, not mine. Or maybe conscience doesn't come into it at all because Bernhard knows about us...or at least should know...or should have to assume it...or should be able to imagine it...or...I don't know, I'm no longer up on your interpretation of "convenience" and openness. I've lost track. No, more than that, I've lost interest. I no longer want to have to vault a permanent hurdle by the name of Bernhard whenever I think of you. Nor do I have to crawl secretly into a hole in Pamela's presence whenever I think of you. I think of you whenever I want to, as often as I want to, and in whichever way I want to. Nothing is stopping me, no-one's holding me back any more. Do you know how liberating that is? Yesterday was like a quantum leap for me. Now I'm able to look upon you as if you were there for me and me alone, as if you'd been created especially for me, as if the Italian restaurant had been opened just for us, as if the table had been deliberately constructed so that our legs could touch underneath it, as if the yellow gorse bush had been planted outside the door to my apartment block just for us, twenty years ago, in the knowledge that it would be in bloom when we kissed and embraced twenty years later.

Seven minutes later

Re:

Your observations are spot on, my love. YESTERDAY I WAS THERE FOR YOU AND FOR YOU ALONE! And that look of yours which held me and me alone, and made everything around us disappear, that look which sees the blooming yellow gorse bush as planted for us alone, the world as created for us, please, please, please don't forget how to use it. Practise it before you sleep, practise it again when you wake up, rehearse it in the mirror. Be sparing in its application, don't waste it on anyone else, protect it from grasping hands and bright sunlight, don't subject it to any danger, be careful not to damage it in transit. And if we see each other again, then unpack it for me! Because that look, my love, it knocks me out, it drives me wild. For that look alone, it was worth waiting for e-mails from you for two and a half years. No-one has ever looked at me like that before, Leo. Like, like, like . . . Leike. Yes. Just like that. That's all I wanted to say. It's meant to be a compliment, by the way, just a little one, my sweet. Did you notice?

Ten minutes later

Re:

Do you know what, Emmi my love? Let's stop for today. It can't get any more beautiful than this. And maybe it can only stay as beautiful as this if we refrain from talking about it for a night.

A big kiss!

Yours,

Leo

(And now I'm going to practise the "like, like, like Leike" look.)

CHAPTER EIGHTEEN

The following evening

Subject: A question

A question for the guardian of silence: For how long were
you planning to stay silent about our beautiful "us"?

Twenty minutes later

Re:

A question for the silence-breaker: Where do the two of us
go from here?

Three minutes later

Re:

That depends on you, Leo dear.

Fifty seconds later

Re:

Not on you, Emmi dear?

One minute later

Re:

No, my love, that's always been your big, fatal mistake, and it's been with you for a large stretch of your journey: it led you erroneously to Boston, and even survived the return journey unscathed; it quickly acclimatized and settled in properly at your side. It clings to you like a leech, Leo. Why don't you shake it off, once and for all.

Forty seconds later

Re:

What are you imagining? Am I supposed to be asking whether you'll come over this evening and stay the night?

Fifty seconds later

Re:

It's got absolutely nothing to do with what I imagine, Leo my dear, I know that already; you can't begin to imagine all the things I've been imagining, even since yesterday. But this time it's all about what YOU'RE imagining. And no, please don't ask me about this evening.

Twenty seconds later

Re:

Why not?

Forty seconds later

Re:

Because I'd have to say no.

Forty seconds later

Re:

Why would you have to?

Fifty seconds later

Re:

Because, because, because. Because I don't want you to think I want to have an affair with you. And, perhaps more importantly: because I don't want to have an affair with you! If it was just going to be an affair, we could have saved ourselves two and a half years of e-mails and thirty-seven cubic metres of words.

Thirty seconds later

Re:

If you don't want an affair, Emmi, what *do* you want?

Forty seconds later

Re:

I want you to express what YOU want!

251

Twenty seconds later

Re:

YOU!

One and a half minutes later

Re:

Bravo, Leo! That came quite spontaneously, straight from the gut, and there it stands, and in big letters, too. But what do you mean by YOU? Reading you? Keeping you at the back of my mind? Carrying you about in my closets of feelings? Keeping you as a special point on my hand? Not losing you? Adoring you? Seeing you? Hearing you? Smelling you? Feeling you? Kissing you? Grabbing you? Pulling you to the floor? Making you pregnant? Eating you up?

One and a half minutes later

Re:

EVERYTHING YOU! (Apart from "making you pregnant", but come to think of it, why not?)

One minute later

Re:

Nice one, Leo! At the very height of your embarrassment, you nonetheless manage to show the beginnings of a sense of humour. But seriously, who is preventing you from doing whatever you want with me? Come on, tell me, where are the two of us going to go from here?

Seven minutes later

Subject: Tell me!

Leeeeoooo! Please! Now is not the time to go all silent again!
Tell me! Write it to me! You can do it! You'll manage! Just
trust yourself! You're so nearly there!

Four minutes later

Re:

O.K., if you're so determined to have what I want in writing,
even though you know it already: Dear Emmi, let's . . . no, do
you want . . . or, can you imagine . . . O.K., it's not about what
you could imagine, it's about what I could imagine. Emmi,
I can imagine that I'd like to make a go of it with you!

Thirty seconds later

Re:

What do you mean by "it"?

Forty seconds later

Re:

The future.

One minute later

Re:

I see the "future" as feminine, and (therefore) totally
unreliable. First let's make a go of "togetherness", I think

253

that would be appropriate, more businesslike, very much an "it". That would be it. Possibly. Probably.

Forty seconds later

Re:

Emmi, I knew ultimately that it would all be about what YOU could imagine! And please tell me the difference between "your" togetherness and "my" affair.

Fifty seconds later

Re:

The aspiration, the intention, the goal. An affair will run its course. Togetherness is staying together, so that we might, at last, have a wonderful life together.

Three minutes later

Re:

Dear Emmi,

O.K., let's imagine staying together in our (planned) togetherness of a wonderful life together. Now, I'm sorry, but I've got to ask this question: Could you imag...Would you separate from Bernhard? Would you get a divorce?

Twenty seconds later

Re:

No.

Forty seconds later

Re:

Alright then, forget it!

Thirty seconds later

Re:

Dear Leo,

Don't just say "Alright then, forget it." Ask me instead:
"Why not?"

Forty seconds later

Re:

Why should I ask you that, Emmi?

Fifty seconds later

Re:

Don't ask why you should be asking me. Ask me instead
why I wouldn't get a divorce!

Thirty seconds later

Re:

Dear Emmi,

I'm not going to have you tell me what I should be asking
you. It's still up to me to ask you what I ask you. So: Why
wouldn't you get a divorce?

Twenty seconds later

Re:

Because I'm already divorced.

Two minutes later

Re:

No!

Twelve minutes later

Re:

Yes, I really am. Since 11.33 a.m. on 17th November, roughly
half a year ago. You may have already wiped this unpleasant
chapter from your memory, but it was around the time of
our three-month break from writing to each other, after my
night-time visit in the fog, after I announced T-H-E E-N-D in
big letters. That was when I moved out. That's when I told
Bernhard everything about us, or rather, about the second
part of our story, the part he didn't already know. That was
when we officially agreed, quite amicably and without
apportioning any blame, that our marriage was no longer in
such great shape, and that it had become stuck in a dreadful
rut. That's when we drew the conclusions. That's when we
separated. Yes, that's how it was. And it was the right thing
to have done. And it was good that we did it. It hurt, but
only a little bit. The children didn't even notice. Nothing
much changed in our daily routine. We stayed together as
a family.

Forty seconds later

Re:

Why did you keep it a secret from me?

One minute later

Re:

I didn't keep it a secret from you, Leo, I just didn't tell you.
It wasn't so, so, so . . . important, yes, it wasn't so important.
Actually it was no more than a formal act. I was going to
mention it at some point. But then "Pam" got in the way. She
was practically there on your doorstep. And then, somehow,
I didn't think it would be appropriate.

Forty seconds later

Re:

But Emmi, you and Bernhard – just the two of you – went
on that idyllic holiday of reconciliation to the Canary
Islands.

Thirty seconds later

Re:

It wasn't an idyllic holiday of reconciliation, it was a
harmonious holiday of convenience. And on a scale of good
holidays, they're about as far apart as you can possibly get
emotionally. We were at peace with one other.

Forty seconds later

Re:

So much at peace that you moved back in with him afterwards. I saw that as an unmistakable sign of the strength of your relationship.

Eight minutes later

Re:

And I saw that as an unmistakable sign of your knack for totally misunderstanding things when there's absolutely no room for misunderstanding! My proposal from La Gomera couldn't have been any more explicit, but you declined it by not listening to it. In true Leo fashion you let the waves surge past you. Ever since we've known each other you've slept through one seventh wave after another, my love.

Forty seconds later

Re:

And that's why you opted for Bernhard and moved back in with him. Where's the misunderstanding in that?

Five minutes later

Re:

No, Leo. We merely resumed our domestic arrangement of living together for a common purpose. It meant I was better able to look after the children when he was on tour. It also meant that I was no longer sitting in the Leo waiting room, staring at the blank walls.

Fifty seconds later

Re:

I didn't know that.

Thirty seconds later

Re:

I know.

Forty seconds later

Re:

All this is new and unfamiliar, but it feels pretty good
to know.

Thirty seconds later

Re:

I'm delighted for you.

Three minutes later

Re:

So what now?

Fifty seconds later

Re:

Now I think I need a whisky.

Thirty seconds later

Re:

And after that?

Two minutes later

Re:

After that you can ask me again whether I'd like to come over to your place. In the meantime you can start practising your gorse-bush look and counting waves.

Five minutes later

Re:

Finished the whisky yet?

Thirty seconds later

Re:

Yes.

Twenty seconds later

Re:

Are you coming?

Fifteen seconds later

Re:

Yes.

Thirty seconds later

Re:

Really?

Twenty seconds later

Re:

Yes.

Twenty-five seconds later

Re:

See you soon.

Twenty seconds later

Re:

Yes.

CHAPTER NINETEEN

Three months later

Subject: (no subject)

Are you online, my sweet? Did I leave my mobile round at yours this morning? Could you have a look? 1.) Dressing-gown pocket. 2.) Black jeans (in the washing basket – hope you haven't washed them yet). 3.) On the chest of drawers in the hall. Best would be if you gave it a call and listened out for it.

Kiss.

E.

Two minutes later

Subject: (no subject)

Don't worry, just found it. Really looking forward to seeing you!!

E.

Three hours later

Re:

Hello darling, lovely to read you! Lovely to write to you. We should do this more often. A thousand kisses. And make sure you're hungry!

See you soon,
Leo

MACLEHOSE PRESS

~ Read the World ~

www.maclehosepress.com

VISIT OUR WEBSITE
OR JOIN US ON TWITTER AND
FACEBOOK FOR:

· Exclusive interviews and films
from MacLehose Press authors

· Exclusive extra material

· Pre-publication sneak previews

· Free chapter samplers and
reading group material

· Competitions and giveaways

And to subscribe to our quarterly newsletter

www.maclehosepress.com
twitter.com/maclehosepress
facebook.com/maclehosepress